D0823341

ORCHIDS OF PASSION

Kit Daly

A CANDLELIGHT SUPREME

Published by
Dell Publishing Co., Inc.
1 Dag Hammarskjold Plaza
New York, New York 10017

Dell ® TM 681510, Dell Publishing Co., Inc.

Candlelight Supreme is a trademark
of Dell Publishing Co., Inc.

Candlelight Ecstasy Romance®, 1,203,540, is a registered
trademark of Dell Publishing Co., Inc., New York, New York.

ISBN: 0-440-16621-7

Printed in the United States of America

August 1987

10 9 8 7 6 5 4 3 2 1

WFH

To Paula.
Thanks for all the hours you listened.

To Our Readers:

We are pleased and excited by your overwhelmingly positive response to our Candlelight Supremes. Unlike all the other series, the Supremes are filled with more passion, adventure, and intrigue and are obviously the stories you like best.

In months to come we will continue to publish books by many of your favorite authors, as well as the very finest work from new authors of romantic fiction. As always, we are striving to present unique, absorbing love stories —the very best love has to offer.

Breathtaking and unforgettable, Supremes follow in the great romantic tradition you've come to expect *only* from Candlelight Romances.

Your suggestions and comments are always welcome. Please let us hear from you.

Sincerely,

The Editors
Candlelight Romances
1 Dag Hammarskjold Plaza
New York, New York 10017

ORCHIDS OF
PASSION

CHAPTER ONE

Suddenly he was running toward the half-consumed hut. He stumbled and fell to the ground, the hard impact knocking his breath away. The smell of the smoke-saturated air made him scramble to his feet. Instantly he was moving forward again, his cry of agony rising above the sounds of the raging flames.

He had to reach his parents.

Michael bolted upright in bed. His eye flew open as sweat streamed down his face, drenching his body. Shudder after shudder racked him as he focused on his safe surroundings—thousands of miles away from the African jungle, decades later.

But the stench of charred wood and burned vegetation seemed to hang in the air like a shroud, and images filled his mind that reminded him of that day thirty years before. It was as though it had happened only yesterday.

No!

Shaking his head violently, Michael whipped back the sheet and stood by the bed. He hadn't had the nightmare in over a year. He wouldn't let it return now to plague him with ghosts from his past. Again he resolved to acknowledge that part of his life and then force it into the background as he had so many times before.

Sunlight poured through the window like liquid gold and caught his attention. He strode to the window and looked out on the promise of another beautiful day in paradise. As he watched, the gray tint of dawn gave way to bright morning light. Beyond the palms and ironwoods he could see two-foot waves pounding the shore relentlessly. They kept returning, like his nightmare.

Why now, when he had finally retired from the State Department? he wondered. Why now, when his life was peaceful and safe? When he was trying to find out what kind of man he really was?

Driven to put distance between himself and his bed, he snatched up a pair of shorts and went into the kitchen to fix some coffee. Then, mug in hand, he went out to the deck that overlooked the beach and ocean. Leaning against the wooden railing, he took a deep breath of the salt-scented air.

Hawaii. Paradise. Peaceful haven for a world-weary man who had seen more than his share of violence and betrayal.

He half sat on the railing, resting his mug on the ledge. He relaxed and tried to allow the tranquillity of the new day seep in and heal. But as always there was a part of him that was wound tight, ready for action at the slightest provocation. Damn. Not even paradise could take that innate wariness away. It had been drilled into him early, when most boys were playing baseball or riding their bikes.

Taking a long sip of coffee, he gazed at the flowering bushes to his left and at the garden beyond, a profusion of beauty that appealed to his aesthetic taste. The riot of color assailed his senses and made him wonder about the people who lived next door among the neatly landscaped grounds.

His colleague in Washington, from whom he had rented the house, had told him only that a man by the name of Lawrence Harris lived there. Whoever he was, he had to love beauty and order, if his garden was any indication of the man.

A movement within the garden suddenly caught his attention. A woman no more than five feet tall stood and rolled her slender shoulders to loosen her muscles. Her straight

13

black hair was bound by a single rubber band and hung almost to her waist. She removed her wide-brimmed hat and fanned herself as she surveyed her gardening.

Michael observed her unobtrusively. He could discover a lot about people when they didn't realize he was watching. The woman's every movement was a graceful extension of the one before it. She was so slightly built that he thought his hands could almost span her waist. Her skin was pale, in stark contrast to her ebony hair. Her features were oriental and yet not. Her almond-shaped eyes were narrowed in study, as if she weren't pleased with whatever she had just done.

Then her head lifted slightly and her dark eyes met his. Time became suspended as they appraised each other across the forty feet that separated them.

When she smiled, her whole face lit up, and Michael couldn't control the quickening of his heartbeat. He purposely brought his mug to his lips to break that spell between them, emotionally distancing himself from her. He was wary of beautiful women; too often in his line of work they proved to be a man's downfall.

When Mei Li Vandenburg had felt someone staring at her, she glanced up to find a man next door looking intently at her. It had been disconcerting, and yet she hadn't been able to resist smiling at him. He seemed so alone, and his features had been devoid of expression.

She was tempted to say something and was about to when she heard Lawrence calling her name. She turned from the man next door to watch Lawrence Harris wheel himself out into the garden, as he did every morning when she was working. She smiled and waved at him.

Then she turned back to see if the man next door was still there. The deck was empty except for the table and chairs, and she wondered if she had imagined him. She hadn't realized the house next door was occupied. It had been vacant for over four months.

She stared at the sliding-glass door that led into the stranger's house and couldn't help feeling disappointed. Who was he?

"What's wrong, Mei Li?" Lawrence asked, braking his wheelchair behind her on the walkway.

She whirled around, startled because for a moment she had forgotton all about Lawrence. "Wrong? Nothing. I was just wondering who was staying next door."

"No one." Lawrence paused, frowning, his gaze drifting to the house in question. "Yes, there is someone staying in Kurt's house. I'd nearly forgotten. Kurt called me a few days ago to tell me that he was renting his house to a Washington colleague for a couple of months. Now let me see. What was his name?" His frown deepened as he thought back to the conversation with his friend. "Ah, I think Kurt said his name was Rutledge and that he used to work for the State Department as a liaison agent. Why do you ask?" His blue eyes fastened on Mei Li.

Her smile reached deep into her black eyes as she gestured with her hands. "I was surprised to see someone on the deck. I'm used to the house being vacant seven or eight months of the year."

Lawrence shook his head. "Such a shame for it to go to waste. I'm glad Kurt is letting someone stay there when he's not using it."

Sounds of Beethoven floated from the house with the stranger named Rutledge living in it to Mei Li on a light breeze. Again she looked toward it. The intense, thundering music seemed to match the man on the deck. She could imagine him on a cliff overlooking the rough sea, braving the harsh elements alone.

"I see you've planted another blue ginger."

Mei Li determinedly turned her attention to Lawrence, who was more like a grandfather to her than an employer. "I wanted more color in this section of the garden, but I'm not quite pleased with this area yet."

"If I know you, you'll have it just right within a week," he said with a laugh. "How are your orchids doing?"

Her face brightened. Orchids were her favorite flower, and she loved to discuss them. "Let me show you."

As Lawrence propelled his motorized wheelchair, Mei Li walked behind him to another section of the garden. She sat on a stone bench in front of Lawrence, and for the next thirty minutes they talked about the different varieties of orchids that Mei Li had cultivated in his garden.

He loved to listen to her talk about the garden and the flowers, loved to watch the way she used her hands to convey her point. There were times he found himself watching her movements more than listening to her softly spoken, melodic words. She had brought a serene beauty into his life, which had been filled only with amassing a fortune for many years. But for what purpose? So his relatives could divide his empire and fight over who got the biggest share after he died?

Lawrence bent forward and took Mei Li's small hand in his. "I'm glad your Uncle Chang talked me into hiring you to plan my garden. You have transformed my home into a paradise within a paradise. It makes having to be confined to this wheelchair much more pleasant."

"Your body may be confined, but your mind isn't."

She placed her other hand over his. When she had first come to the Harris house more than two years before, this dear old man had been dispirited and mean-tempered because the doctors had told him he would be in a wheelchair for the rest of his life.

The first month she had been there, Mei Li had quickly discovered that she couldn't accept someone shutting himself up in his house. She had practically bullied Lawrence into coming outside to see her labors. That was when they had begun their morning ritual of visiting for an hour or so. At first they had talked about the garden, but now their conversations encompassed many subjects. Lawrence had seen and done so much more than she. He had opened up a new world for her, giving her as much as she gave him.

Suddenly Lawrence frowned, his look intense, probing. "You haven't regretted coming to work for me, have you?"

"Regret? Working in this garden?" She gestured at the beauty around them. "Because of you I work full time doing something I love. How could I regret that?" She had taken the grounds surrounding his house and transformed them into a garden that rivaled long-established gardens on the island. Everytime she walked among the flowers, pride swelled within her.

"I know of your family's disapproval." His fingers clasped the arms of his wheelchair; the veins in the back of his hands protruded tautly.

The light in her eyes died. "Why is my father so against you?" Though she had needed the job, her parents had been vehemently against her working for Lawrence. But now even her father didn't say anything about it to her anymore. He silently accepted her employer, but he never asked about her work at the Harris house.

"Have you asked him why?"

"Yes, but he won't say." She didn't understand her father's continual refusal not to tell her because both her parents had always been straightforward with their children.

"Then I will respect his silence, Mei Li. The explanation must come from your father."

"But—"

Lawrence held up his hand. "Sh. No more. Let's just say that as a powerful, wealthy man, I have collected my share of enemies."

Her brow creased. "Enemies? That's such a strong word."

"But true. Over the years I've stepped on a number of toes. I haven't always been this nice." He grinned, a mischievous gleam in his eyes.

Mei Li started to tease him when a tall man appeared behind Lawrence. She swallowed her words.

"There you are. I've been looking all over the garden." John Harris looked from his father to Mei Li, his gaze sweeping down her length in a heated appraisal.

She shivered but refused to allow the young man to intimidate her.

"I need to talk with you, Father, about business." He started to walk back toward the house but stopped when he realized his father wasn't following him.

The older man waved his hand. "Speak. I'm not ready to go back inside. This day is much too beautiful to be inside."

John pointedly looked at Mei Li. "I need to speak with you in private, Father."

"I don't have any secrets from Mei Li."

Mei Li hid her surprise behind a bland expression, diverting her gaze from John. It was true that Lawrence shared his troubles with her because she had taken the time to listen, but Lawrence was deliberately needling his son. He had told her on several occasions that John was too serious and too wrapped up in the family's real estate business. Lawrence had also told her that his son had accused Mei Li of being after his father's money; this was a cardinal sin, because to John money was everything.

John's frown strengthened into a scowl. "Then this can wait until later. Excuse me." He stormed away before Lawrence could say anything else.

"I wish you wouldn't use me as bait," Mei Li gently scolded.

"I have two pleasures in life since my confinement to this thing," he said, indicating his wheelchair. "One is you and this garden. With you I don't have to be one of the richest men in Hawaii. I don't have to prove anything to you."

"And the other?"

"Baiting my son. He has too much starch in his shirts."

Mei Li laughed. "Do you purposely give him the wrong impression of us?"

"No, I'd never do that to you. My son reads our friendship the wrong way all by himself."

"Oh, you are incorrigible!"

"Yes, I know. Being wealthy and old gives me a few privileges."

"Chang would say being wealthy and old gives you a few added responsibilities."

"Yes, your uncle would say that," Lawrence replied with a grin.

"Mr. Harris, it's time for your medication," the nurse, Mrs. Duncan, said as she entered the alcove in the garden.

Lawrence bent forward and whispered to Mei Li, "No doubt John ran inside and solicited Mrs. Duncan's help."

"I should get back to work. I have to be over at the Maxwells' this afternoon to make sure everything is set for their lawn party this evening."

"I give you a break, and now you're in demand everywhere. I wish I'd never told the Maxwells about you," Lawrence grumbled as Nancy Duncan led the way toward the house.

Mei Li remained on the bench a moment, watching Lawrence and his nurse until they disappeared from her view. Because of Lawrence she had more work than she knew what to do with. She was employed as his full-time gardener as well as the Maxwells', but often their friends asked for her help and advice. She found her days very busy, but that was the way she preferred it.

Her evenings were spent with her large family or in the greenhouse that her father had built for her in the backyard. She spent little time in the small apartment she rented near her parents' house. Her family didn't understand why she even bothered to return home to it each night. But it was hers, and being from a big family—she had two brothers and three sisters—Mei Li valued her privacy. She tried to make them realize that although she loved her family and being with them, she loved her independence, too.

Mei Li rose and made her way back to the blue ginger to finish her task. Charlie, her oldest brother, would arrive soon to take her to the Maxwells. She hated it when her station wagon acted up. If she didn't know better, she would think her car had a mind of its own and knew when she was too busy to fool with it.

After she completed her task, she took her tools to the shed. As she was leaving, she collided with John in the doorway. He blocked her exit, forcing her to step back into the dimly lit shed.

"It seems to me you spend more time talking to my father than doing your job," John taunted.

She refused to respond to that comment. She remained where she was, outwardly serene while inside she was trembling with anger.

"If you think you'll get any of his money when he dies, just remember, I can be a powerful adversary. I won't let anything happen to Harris Enterprises, including my father's folly." He left as quickly as he had appeared.

Mei Li shuddered. She had never been threatened before; she wasn't sure how to handle it. Uncle Chang would advise calm patience, but in the face of John's anger it was hard to practice that.

She decided to forget the incident. She wouldn't add to the deteriorating relationship between Lawrence and his son. Perhaps John was just frustrated with his father and taking it out on her.

As she walked around the side of the house to wait for her brother out front, her gaze wandered to the house next door. The shutters were closed, and the house was silent. The man named Rutledge seemed to be gone. She wondered what his first name was and how long he would be next door.

As she stood at the end of the driveway, she glanced at her watch several times, berating her brother for being late, which was usual for him. Frustrated because out of her large family Charlie was the only one who could pick her up, she began to walk in the direction he would come. When she heard a car approaching, she looked up, sure it would be Charlie. But the car was a white Mercedes coupe.

Disappointed, she started to look away; then she realized that the stranger from next door was driving. He stopped several feet away from Mei Li, leaned over, and rolled down the window.

"Is something wrong?" he asked, his voice like sandpaper sliding over silk.

She shook her head, her gaze riveted to the compelling man before her. His dark brown eyes and sun-streaked hair combined with his sharp features to give an impression of ruthlessness, and yet she sensed an air of vulnerability about him. "I'm just waiting for a ride. Thanks for asking."

When she smiled at him, Michael did something impulsive, which was totally unlike him. "May I give you a lift somewhere?"

She paused, glanced up the street, then answered, "No, I'd better wait for my brother. If I'm not here when he finally shows up I'll never hear the end of it."

One part of Michael was relieved that she had turned down the ride; he didn't want to get involved. The other part was disappointed, and he was finding it difficult to suppress that feeling.

"Fine. I hope your brother comes soon." Michael rolled the window back up, pulled into his driveway, and parked in front of his house.

Taking a look at his rearview window, he watched the woman walk away. His disappointment grew stronger as he followed her with his eyes. She was dressed in jeans that hugged her slender curves provocatively. Her flowered print shirt was tied at the waist, emphasizing her slim waist. She was petite, like a china doll, Michael reflected as he climbed from his car.

His gaze immediately veered to the woman, and he swore beneath his breath. Damnation! He was attracted to her, and he knew he shouldn't be. Determinedly he jerked his gaze away and strode into the house. His whole life was up in the air, and he certainly didn't need added complications. He was forty years old and didn't know what he wanted to do with the rest of his life. But one thing was certain: he wasn't emotionally or mentally ready for any kind of relationship.

He had tried a relationship once, and it had nearly destroyed him—and Laura. The real problem was that Michael didn't know how to trust another person; that ability had died in him a long time ago. He was a loner, always had been and probably always would be. And yet that inability to trust was why he had been so good at his job.

The next morning, before work, Mei Li paused at the edge of the beach and stared at the sky, tinted with an array of bright colors.

Sunrise, the beginning to a new day, was always her favorite time.

The salt-permeated breeze tugged at the strands of her long hair. The cool touch of it felt good against her bare arms. She closed her eyes and breathed deeply; the air was laced with the fresh scent of flowers from Lawrence's garden, her creation.

A sound disturbed her tranquillity, and she opened her eyes to find the man from next door jogging toward the water. He entered the surf and dove into a large wave. He broke through the surface and tossed his head, shaking the water off his hair. Then with long purposeful strokes he made his way out to sea.

Transfixed, Mei Li stared at him, telling herself she was only staying in case anything happened to the man. People shouldn't swim alone, she had been taught, especially where there was an undertow. But in truth, even if there had been other people on the beach, she would have remained.

She wasn't sure why he fascinated her, but for some reason she was intrigued by the stranger. He seemed to stand apart from everyone else, as if he had no one in the world to care about him. For someone like herself, who came from a large, loving family, that was a hard concept to accept. Or maybe she was attracted to him because they seemed to be opposites. He seemed so tough, and she suspected he would be capable of handling any dangerous situation he found himself in.

When he emerged from the water, Mei Li stepped back into the shadows of the ironwoods and continued to study the man boldly. As he ran a towel over his body, her gaze was drawn from his muscular arms to his broad chest, then down to his long powerful legs. He was in superb condition, which reinforced her conviction that he could take care of himself.

He placed the towel about his neck and began to jog down the beach toward her. For a few seconds she panicked, not wanting him to discover her and the way she had blatantly spied on him. She felt like a deer trapped in the headlights of a car.

She glanced around, but it was too late. He had seen her and was heading straight for her. She took another step back, wishing the ironwoods would swallow her up. It was totally out of character for her to admire a man so brazenly.

"Good morning." He smiled, a slow lifting of the corners of his mouth. "Did your brother ever come yesterday?"

She nodded; his warm smile soothed her. "Ten minutes later, with a hundred excuses for being late." She made a valiant effort to relax her tense body.

"Did you let him off the hook?" The corners of his dark brown eyes crinkled as his smile deepened.

Her eyes flashed with her own smile. "Yes. It does no good to try to reform my older brother. He'll always be late for everything." She held out her hand. "My name is Mei Li Vandenburg."

"Michael Rutledge." He took her small hand in his and shook it, reluctant to let it go.

He hadn't been able to resist talking to her when he had seen her standing in the grove of ironwoods. He should have jogged away from her—there were a thousand reasons why he should have, but her delicate figure and porcelain features had drawn him closer.

Mei Li slipped her hand from his, wishing there were a reason for him to hold it longer. But her mind refused to function. His warm grasp had been a strange combination of strength and gentleness and had sent her heartbeat galloping.

There was a moment of silence, when only the sounds of the surf and birds could be heard, as they stood a foot apart and stared at each other.

Finally Michael broke the silence by asking, "Do you work for Lawrence Harris?"

She nodded, swallowing to coat her dry throat. "I'm the gardener." She glanced toward the house next door. "Have you been here long?" She thought of all the questions she would have preferred to ask him but had no right to.

"Five days."

Five days, and she hadn't known it until yesterday! There hadn't been any sign that someone was living at the McNeils'. Was he hiding from the world? Instead she asked, "Are you going to be staying long?"

He shrugged. "I'm not sure."

That was his problem: he wasn't sure about anything. All his life he had had direction until now. Suddenly he was reminded of the first day he had been stranded in the jungle as a child of ten, having to cope with survival all alone.

Beads of sweat broke out on his forehead as the memory shook him. Why did he have to remember now? Because he had been spending the last thirty years running away from himself, and now he had the time to face the past, to face those ghosts? Time and idleness seemed to be his enemies.

"Are you all right?" Mei Li automatically stepped forward, cutting the distance between them in half. The shaken expression on

30

his suddenly pale face alarmed her, and she reached out to him.

He took a step back, his features shuttered. "Yes. I just remembered I have something to do. Good day, Miss Vandenburg," he replied in a polite, strained voice as he backed farther away, then turned and jogged toward his house.

Mei Li watched him go. She couldn't shake the feeling that Michael Rutledge was a driven man, torn into pieces and desperately trying to put the fragments back together. She sensed that she could help him, but she somehow doubted he would let her get close enough to try.

CHAPTER TWO

Mei Li slid into the front seat of the Volks-
wagen. "Thanks for the lift, Charlie."

Her oldest brother chuckled. "You aren't
angry that I'm late—again?"

"No, that's to be expected," she replied,
and smiled. She was learning that the only
way to handle her brother's perpetual tardi-
ness was to tell him to pick her up earlier than
she needed the ride. Chang had told her that
people don't change unless they really want
to, and she had discovered that Charlie didn't
care if he was late. He was oblivious to the
people around him. Cars were the only thing
that he cared about besides his family.

"You don't mind if we stop by the Harris
place for an hour while I work on one of his
cars?"

"No, I always have things to do there." Her
mind wasn't on the garden but on the house
next door and the man who occupied it. Their

encounter that morning on the beach had left her very curious about Michael Rutledge.

"Right before I came, Dad and I had words over my working for Lawrence Harris." Charlie's voice cut into her thoughts.

Mei Li looked at her brother. "Words? I gather angry ones." She had recommended her brother as a mechanic to Lawrence, because with three children and a pregnant wife to support Charlie needed the extra money.

"You gather right. I stopped by Dad's boat to try and fix his engine. When I told him I had to leave, he asked me why, since the engine still isn't running." Charlie glanced at her. "Mei Li, I don't think it's ever going to run properly. Or if I manage to repair it, it won't last long. He needs a new engine."

"Everything is falling apart. He needs a new boat."

"Which he can't afford. I wish I could help him, but I have my own family to feed. You know that's the only reason I agreed to work on Mr. Harris's cars. I realize Dad was never keen on the idea of you working for Mr. Harris." He blew out a breath of air. "But until today I didn't realize how much."

"Dad feels betrayed by Lawrence."

Charlie nodded. "Why? What's between

those two? You know Mr. Harris. Does he say anything?"

"Nothing. If we want to know, it has to come from Dad."

Charlie frowned. "Then I'll ask Dad."

"He won't tell you. I've tried."

"I'll find a way. If he has a good reason why I shouldn't work for Mr. Harris, then I won't. But he's going to have to tell me before I walk away from money I can use."

"And you think I should give up my job if there's a good reason?"

The look in his eyes sharpened. "When you get right down to it, family is all we have. It's the most important thing and should come first."

"You're saying I should disregard my friendship with Lawrence?" Lawrence was the first person in her life that she felt needed her, and she knew she couldn't just walk away because of something in the past between him and her father. Whatever it was was between Lawrence and her father, not her and Lawrence, or for that matter her brother and Lawrence.

"I realize you're caught in the middle. You'll have to make up your own mind," Charlie said as he pulled into the Harris driveway.

Mei Li opened her door. "I'll be out in the

garden, the rose section. Come and get me when you're through." She started to climb from the car when her brother grabbed her arm.

"I need the money, but you must realize, we're all Dad has. He's always been there for us."

"Money has nothing to do with why I stay, Charlie." She pulled her arm free and slipped from the car. "Loyalty is important, I agree. But don't let it blind you to the whole picture."

As she walked toward the rose garden, she felt frustrated. Sometimes her family demanded too much of her. They wanted to live her life for her, to dictate what she should do and whom she should see. It was at times like this when she needed to escape them and be alone. Being the youngest in a large family left very little for her to do. She felt as if she were being swallowed up and becoming a part of a large whole with no identity of her own.

But when she was with Lawrence or working in his garden, she didn't feel that way. In the two years she had worked for him, she had discovered herself. She was content and pleased with the pattern of her life. No, she wouldn't walk away from him as long as he needed her friendship. She refused to let

35

Charlie upset her. Calm patience—she reminded herself of Chang's teaching. Everything would work out in the end.

As Michael read the letter from Mark Prince, a smile mitigated the severity of his rugged features. Mark and Anna were to be married at the end of the month, and they wanted him to attend the wedding. Mark had worked with him on his last case for the State Department in Austria. It was seeing Mark fall in love with Anna that had made Michael realize how empty his life was. He had avoided any kind of permanent relationship because of his job, and now he felt he had to still because he didn't know what the hell he wanted. He wondered if he had spent too many years living on the outside looking in, but it seemed too late to change that now.

Michael laid the letter on the coffee table in front of him. That last case had also underscored his growing disillusionment. He had lost a good friend and agent in that operation. For the first time he had felt his age and had realized that after sixteen years with the government he had little to show for them, aside from a sizable savings portfolio and various scars from encounters with the opposing side.

The phone rang. Michael snatched up the

receiver before the second ring. "Rutledge here."

"How's Hawaii? Bored yet?"

"In paradise?" Michael chuckled.

"I was just wondering if you were climbing the walls of my house yet."

"Kurt, I doubt very seriously that you're taking the time to call about my recreational activities. What's up?"

"We have an interesting job that I thought you might like to know about—that is, if you're through vacationing."

"I'm through, period. Remember that resignation I turned in a few weeks ago? You should know me by now. It takes awhile for me to make up my mind, but once I do, I don't change it. I never do anything on impulse." Well, almost never, he amended silently as he remembered Mei Li and the ride he had offered her.

"It has to do with a terrorist group in Colombia. I know how you feel about so-called revolutionary armies."

For a brief moment Michael's mind flashed back to a "soldier" in a revolutionary army who pointed his gun at his mother's head. His breath caught, and he struggled to drag air into his lungs.

"Michael? Are you still there?"

"Yes, Kurt. And no to your offer. I really am

through." The quiet steel in his voice emphasized his declaration.

"I had to try. You'd be the best man for the job. If you change your mind—."

"I won't. Good-bye, Kurt."

Michael hung up, but his hand lingered on the receiver as he stared at the floor, fighting the image of his parents and the soldiers. Finally he was able to clear his mind of them. He put a Brahms recording on the stereo and let the soft music soothe his soul.

At the window his gaze instinctively sought the peaceful garden next door. He searched for Mei Li among its beauty, hoping to see her again. Their sunrise conversation had haunted him all day and had left him wanting to know more about the woman. She reminded him of a plant he had run across in the Amazon jungle. Its beauty was compelling, but its touch deadly.

He saw Mei Li kneeling and tilling the earth in the rose garden. Why was he always drawn back to her? Immediately he knew the answer: it was her gentle serenity. It was so different from the brutal violence of his life. His uncle had raised him after his parents' death, but then his job had robbed him of any normalcy in his life. He wondered if it were even possible to erase the harsh cynicism that was so much a part of him.

Watching Mei Li so lovingly tending the flowers, he doubted it. What was the saying? An old dog couldn't be taught new tricks? He turned away from the window and Mei Li. No, he was who he was, and he wasn't going to change at forty. He was going to have to learn to adapt to the world of polite society, but he doubted he would ever truly be part of it.

The late afternoon sun slanted through the palm trees and bathed Mei Li in its warmth. The soft breeze caressed her face, and the sweet fragrance of the roses mingled with the fresh sea air and teased her senses.

She was working the earth around the rosebushes; her actions were automatic. No matter how much she tried to forget her brother's words, they kept returning. What if her father had a good reason for hating Lawrence? What should she do? Why did her father keep it a secret?

Questions with no answers swirled in her thoughts. She wasn't being disloyal to her father; she had to live her own life and do what was best for her. All her life in her large family she had fought for her own place. But still guilt plagued her as she jabbed her spade into the ground and flipped the dirt over, not really aware of what she was doing.

"I never thought about taking my frustrations out on the ground. Does it work?" a deep voice, full of amusement, asked.

Mei Li gasped at the sudden intrusion. Her gaze rose until it rested on Michael's smiling face. "It's great therapy. You should try it sometime."

His smile deepened. "You may have something there. I just might."

Mei Li sat back on her heels, shading her eyes with her hand. "Mr. McNeil could use a gardener."

Laughter rolled from Michael's throat. "I'll have to tell him. I can't imagine Kurt working outdoors more than five minutes."

"No, neither can I." Mei Li dusted off her pants and started to rise, deciding she was definitely at a disadvantage looking up at Michael with his back to the sun.

He held his hand out to her, and she took it, liking the contrasting sensations his grasp created. The rough texture of his skin was in opposition to his gentle touch.

"It's hard, though, to look at his grounds and not want to do something with them." Being so close to Michael again made Mei Li nervous. She quickly withdrew her hand from his.

"I have some time on my hands." Now that was an understatement, he thought. He had more time than he knew what to do with.

"Maybe I could do something with the place —if you'd give me some advice."

"Do you know anything about gardening?"

"What's to know? Don't you just plant a bush, water it, and pick the flowers when they bloom?"

Mei Li's brow wrinkled. "If that's what you think, you have a lot to learn."

"Well, I must confess I never really thought about it. I don't think I've ever even had a houseplant."

"Not even one?" It was hard for Mei Li to comprehend a person not having at least one plant, when her whole apartment was filled with them.

"In my job I traveled a lot. The plant would have died from lack of attention." Like any relationship he would have had, Michael realized. "I thought it best not to have any. Who wants to return home to a dead plant?"

"You're right. A garden takes time and attention." Mei Li sensed their conversation was taking on a double meaning. Michael's brooding intensity was almost palpable.

"And isn't cultivated in a day or a week."
For a long moment they stared at each other; the air was electric, as if a thunderstorm were brewing. The usual shutter over Michael's expression was gone for that brief moment, and the atmosphere was charged

41

with his needs. Mei Li reached toward him, her fingertips inches from his arm.

Suddenly Michael's head jerked up; his sharp gaze narrowed on a place behind Mei Li. Then, before she had a chance to turn around to see what he was looking at, he sprang forward and raced toward the house.

Confusion held her immobile for a few seconds. Sensing that something was terribly wrong, she hurried after Michael. She arrived at the swimming pool just as Michael dived into the deep end and dragged Lawrence to the surface. His wheelchair was floating in the water near the edge.

Fear gripped her as she watched Michael pull Lawrence to the surface and swim with him to the side. She finally moved when Michael tried to lift Lawrence up onto the concrete. She rushed over to help Michael with Lawrence's heavy and lifeless body.

Her heartbeat accelerated when she looked at Lawrence. His eyes were shut, his face colorless. She tried to swallow, to say something, but her throat closed painfully around the words.

Michael hauled himself from the water and immediately began giving Lawrence mouth-to-mouth resuscitation. Mei Li silently prayed as she watched and waited for a sign of life. Her heart felt as if it would explode.

Then suddenly Lawrence began to cough and spit up water. She had never heard a more wonderful sound. His eyelids fluttered open. His gaze focused first on Michael, then Mei Li, and half-smile touched his quivering lips.

Michael moved back to let Mei Li come around to Lawrence's side. She laid her hand on his arm and smiled down at the older man, who was shivering even though it was hot.

"I thought the doctor told you to give up swimming," she said.

Her statement provoked a small laugh from Lawrence.

"What happened, Lawrence?" Mei Li asked, trying to keep concern from her voice.

"I'm not sure. It happened so fast." His voice was weak.

"Well, the important thing is that you're all right. We'll get you inside and call the doctor."

"I don't need the doctor. Just took in a little water," Lawrence grumbled. His voice was growing stronger.

"Then humor me. I want to make sure everything is fine." Her voice caught. "Please."

"I suppose if I don't, John or Madge will insist."

"Good." Mei Li glanced over her shoulder at Michael. "Can you get his wheelchair?"

"Later. I'll carry him inside and come back for it. He needs to get warm." Michael knelt beside Lawrence and slid his arms under the older man's body. "By the way, I'm your neighbor, Michael Rutledge."

"Lucky for me you were nearby."

Without a word Michael effortlessly lifted Lawrence and carried him toward the house.

With a glance at the wheelchair still in the pool, Mei Li followed, acknowledging that if Michael hadn't been in the garden with her, Lawrence would be dead right now. She hadn't heard anything when Michael had headed for the pool. And even if she had, she wasn't sure she could have pulled Lawrence out of the water in time.

Inside, Lawrence directed Michael to the den, where Michael placed the older man on the couch, then covered him with a blanket.

"I'll get you some dry clothes," Mei Li said, then hurried up to Lawrence's bedroom.

After bringing Lawrence a set of dry clothes, Mei Li left the den so Michael could help Lawrence change. She made the call to the doctor in the study. As she hung up, Madge Harris breezed into the room. A frown marred her face, preserved by cosmetic surgery.

"What's going on here? Who's that strange man in the den with Lawrence? Why are you in the study?" All Madge's haughty disdain was evident in the questions she fired at Mei Li.

Mei Li gave a patient look to Lawrence's daughter-in-law and replied, "Lawrence had an accident. He fell into the pool. That strange man saved his life."

"Lawrence has no business going out to the pool every day. Now maybe he'll listen to me and stop trying to be so damned stubborn. After all, he's an invalid. He should start acting like one."

Mei Li gritted her teeth and kept her mouth shut. The few times that Madge had bothered to speak to her, it had always been an order to do something in the garden or to have a special bouquet for a house party.

Madge had been living with Lawrence ever since his eldest son had died five years before. Her husband had been a reckless gambler, leaving Madge penniless and dependent on Lawrence for her own support as well as her daughter's. Mei Li was glad she had little to do with both Madge and her daughter, Caroline.

"You didn't tell me why you were in the study," Madge said.

"I was calling the doctor." Mei Li walked from around the desk and across the study to the door. The air was becoming unbearably stifling in the room.

"Well, now that I'm here, I can take care of Father. I'm sure you have something to do in the garden." Madge waltzed past her and out the door as if she were royalty and no one could leave a room before her.

"No, I don't," Mei Li replied in a quiet voice. She had no intention of leaving until she was sure Lawrence would be all right.

Madge's gaze fastened onto Mei Li's determined face, and she said airily, "Suit yourself. You can wait in the hallway until the doctor is through. Or better yet, Caroline ought to know about her grandfather's accident. She's up in her room, the first door on the right." Madge entered the den, dismissing Mei Li with the order.

It would do no good to lose her temper. The only person it would hurt was herself, Mei Li decided. She took a few moments to compose herself, then mounted the stairs.

When she knocked on Caroline's door, Mei Li wondered why the young woman hadn't heard the commotion out at the pool. Her window overlooked that section of the grounds.

"Come in."

Mei Li opened the door and peered into the room. Caroline sat on the canopy bed, cross-legged, with a set of earphones on her head. That might explain why she hadn't heard anything, Mei Li thought as she advanced into the room.

Caroline pulled the earphones off and looked sulkily at Mei Li.

It taxed all of Mei Li's patience not to turn around and leave. She returned Caroline's stare with her own direct regard. Mei Li allowed the silence to lengthen, stressing more than words that Caroline couldn't intimidate her. Caroline was only five years younger than she was, and yet Mei Li couldn't relate to the other woman at all. Caroline accepted the comforts her grandfather offered but protested with her group of friends how her grandfather made his money—through land development in Hawaii.

"Your mother wanted you to know that your grandfather had an accident," Mei Li said finally.

Caroline continued to look at Mei Li for a few more seconds, then slipped the earphones back onto her head, saying, "You've told me, now you can leave."

Mei Li suppressed her impulse to snatch the earphones off Caroline's head and demand a response other than cold indifference. Chang had painstakingly taught her the art of remaining calm and in control of her emotions during times of stress, which she usually managed to accomplish. But Mei Li had to acknowledge that even Chang would have had a hard time in the face of Lawrence's relatives.

Mei Li mustered all her inner dignity and left the room quietly. In the hallway she drew in several deep breaths before heading back downstairs to face Madge again. From the top of the stairs she saw Michael lounging against the newel at the bottom.

He looked up, and his gaze locked with hers. A grin flirted with the corners of his mouth as she descended. Her eyes never left his face.

"I've been coolly dismissed by a woman who says she's Lawrence's daughter." Michael shoved himself away from the newel and stepped into Mei Li's path.

"Daughter-in-law." Even on the bottom stair Mei Li wasn't eye level with Michael. She lifted her gaze to his and felt engulfed by his male essence. There was something elemental about him, a bold recklessness that laughed in the face of danger.

"I got the distinct impression that I was ruining the carpet by dripping all over it." He leaned closer, drawn toward Mei Li, even though his common sense warned him to escape before he got in over his head.

"She fancies herself the mistress of the house." Her words came out in a breathless rush as her pulse hammered through her body.

"She plays that role to the hilt. Oh, she politely thanked me as she escorted me to the front door, but she made it quite clear that she thought I was a servant or some other low specimen of life. I decided to wait." His expression became serious. "I retrieved Lawrence's wheelchair from the pool. The brakes don't work." He couldn't dismiss the uneasy sensation at the nape of his neck that he got when something wasn't quite right. He realized that brakes did fail, but in his line of work he had been taught never to disregard any possibility.

"Lawrence must have come off the ramp into the pool area and not been able to stop." She was having a hard time thinking straight with Michael so close. His nearness assailed her senses and made her skin tingle.

"Does he go out to the pool often?"

"Every day at the same time. He likes to sun himself in the late afternoon after his nap. It's his time to get in touch with himself. No one is allowed to disturb him during that hour."

Again Michael felt that uneasiness along the back of his neck. He rubbed his nape and asked, "He never changes his routine?"

Mei Li tilted her head to the side. "Only when it rains. Why?"

He shrugged. "No particular reason. I've always had a curious streak. Since Lawrence can't swim, I wondered why he was out by the pool."

"That's the best place for the sun at this time of day, and the view is beautiful from the pool deck."

"Yes, but there aren't any places on his grounds that aren't beautiful."

Blushing at his compliment, Mei Li lowered her gaze. "Beauty is important to Lawrence."

"And you?"

She reestablished eye contact with him and felt trapped by his probing gaze. "I'm no different from the next person. I like beautiful things, but what I consider beautiful, you may not."

"Ah yes, beauty is in the eye of the beholder."

"There isn't anything in nature that I don't marvel at—even what some people would consider ugly."

One corner of his mouth curved upward. "Then snakes and rats don't frighten you."

"Why should they? I do have a healthy respect for them, but they're necessary in the scheme of things."

He moved even closer, his mouth inches from hers. Mei Li's heartbeat stopped as her breath caught.

They both jumped back when the doorbell rang, surprised by the intrusion into what had become their private world. He turned toward the front door as the bell rang again.

"Must be the doctor," Mei Li said as she stepped around Michael and made her way across the spacious foyer to answer the door. Her heart still wasn't beating normally as she swung the door open to admit Dr. Benson. "He's in the den. Mrs. Harris is with him now."

Dr. Benson asked about Lawrence's condition as he walked toward the den. Michael answered his questions.

Mei Li was about to close the front door when Charlie appeared in the doorway.

"Ready to go?" her brother asked.

"I can't right now."

"Mei Li, I have to be at the shop in twenty minutes." Charlie glanced at his watch and amended, "No, make that fifteen minutes."

"Lawrence had an accident. Can't you wait? I want to see how he's doing."

"Accident?"

"He fell into the swimming pool."

"How in the world did that happen?" Charlie asked, astonished.

"His brakes failed," Michael replied as he approached them and extended his hand toward Mei Li's brother. "I'm Michael Rutledge, the next-door neighbor."

Charlie shook Michael's hand. "I'm Charlie Vandenburg." Then he turned to his sister and continued, "Sorry, Mei Li. I can't wait."

"I'll drive you home, Mei Li," Michael said as the door to the den opened and Madge rushed from the room, frowning.

Before Madge could say anything, Charlie said, "Good. I'll be going." He escaped as Madge descended on Mei Li and Michael.

"My brother is definitely a chicken when it comes to Madge Harris," Mei Li whispered to Michael.

Michael chuckled softly, which made Madge's frown strengthen into a scowl.

"Are you two still here?" Her gaze flitted from Mei Li to Michael and then back to Mei Li.

Mei Li squared her shoulders and met the hostility in the older woman's question with quiet dignity. "As you can see, yes. I want to see how Lawrence is doing before I leave."

Nonplussed by Mei Li's reply, Madge fluttered her hand in the air. "He's fine. He's a tough old coot. No doubt he'll be up and about tomorrow, business as usual." Venom was barely concealed behind her neutral expression.

"Nevertheless, I'll wait until Dr. Benson is through."

"Suit yourself. I have other things I must see to."

After Madge left the foyer, Mei Li wanted to sag against Michael's strength. Encounters with that woman always left Mei Li feeling drained emotionally.

"What's taking Dr. Benson so long?" Mei Li asked.

Michael smiled. "I can certainly understand why you would want to leave this house. That woman is less than the gracious hostess."

"Oh, she can be that when she wants to be. When she turns on the charm with Lawrence, I think she missed her calling. She should have been in the movies. Surely Lawrence sees right through her performance but—" Mei Li halted in midsentence. A movement on the stairs caught her attention.

Dressed in a skimpy bikini with a towel slung over her shoulder, Caroline descended the staircase. "Well, how's Granddaddy?" Her gaze was fixed on Michael, and she headed straight for him, completely ignoring Mei Li. "I'm Caroline Harris. Are you a friend of Granddaddy's?"

"I live next door."

An imp surfaced, and Mei Li couldn't resist interrupting. "The doctor is still with Lawrence."

Still not acknowledging Mei Li's presence, Caroline stepped closer to Michael, looking up at him through half-veiled eyes. "Maybe when Dr. Benson is through, you could come tell me if Granddaddy will be all right. I'll be out by the pool"—she paused seductively—"waiting for you."

Michael didn't say a word as Caroline walked off. Mei Li wanted to ask if he was going to see Caroline, but she had no right to. She knew how much Caroline loved to play games with people, and she couldn't see a smart man like Michael falling for any of them.

"Lawrence has an—interesting family. Are there any more?" Michael asked, breaking the silence.

"Only John, his son, who runs the business now. He usually doesn't come home until late. He breathes, eats, and sleeps Harris Enterprises."

"A workaholic. I've been there."

Mei Li started to ask him about that when the door to the den opened and Dr. Benson advanced into the foyer. "Is he all right?"

54

Dr. Benson shook his head, indicating how trying Lawrence could be. "It'll take more than a swim in the pool to keep Lawrence down. He's barking orders as usual. He wants to see you two."

The first thing that Lawrence said when they stepped into the den was "I didn't think Madge would succeed in running you off."

Mei Li noticed the pallor beneath Lawrence's tanned features, but she didn't say anything. He hated to admit to imperfect health.

"Just wanted to see if you both would join me for lunch tomorrow." Lawrence's voice was gruff, but his eyes sparkled with warmth.

Mei Li nodded, while Michael said, "Yes."

"Good. I eat on the terrace at twelve sharp." Lawrence closed his eyes, but as Mei Li and Michael turned to leave the den, Lawrence added, "And thanks, you two."

Until Mei Li shut the door on Lawrence alive and well, she hadn't allowed herself to feel the exhaustion the last hour had caused. Now she leaned back against the wood, inhaling deeply.

Michael turned back toward her and saw her relief and weariness. Without even thinking, he drew her into his embrace and felt her shudder. In that instant he realized how

55

much he had missed by not being in any one place long enough to develop a friendship with another human being. His life seemed very empty.

CHAPTER THREE

Mei Li pulled back from Michael's embrace. "Thanks. I needed to be hugged."

He grinned, her candor delightfully refreshing for someone who had lived in a world of deception. "Anytime. Are you ready to leave now?"

"Yes."

"Good. I'll just change. It won't take me long."

The imp resurfaced in Mei Li. "What about Caroline? She's waiting for you."

"The best way to answer her is to ignore her."

"I have another way."

His grin broadened and one dark brow arched. "While I change, you could give her the news about her grandfather?"

"Right. I see we think along the same lines."

"Why, Mei Li, I didn't know you could be so devious."

"It doesn't pay to rant and rave at someone like Caroline. She would just tune you out and never get your message."

He clasped her elbow as they started for the back of the house. "I do like your style, lady. I'll meet you in front of my house in five minutes."

Mei Li watched Michael cross the lawn. He moved quickly, surely. The fluid grace of his lean frame attested to his superb physical condition. Not until he entered his house did Mei Li finally make her way to the pool.

Caroline had unfastened her bikini bra and was lying on her stomach on a lounge chair. When Mei Li approached, the younger woman held up a bottle of suntan lotion. "Would you please put some on my back?" She asked without looking up.

Her request was laced with purring sounds, having been artfully practiced on men. Mei Li had witnessed this scene before while working in the garden. She suppressed a laugh and took the bottle from Caroline. Squirting some cold lotion onto Caroline's back, Mei Li began to rub it into her skin.

Caroline shot up and twisted about to glare at her. "What the hell are you doing here?"

Mei Li straightened, smiling sweetly. "You wanted to know about your grandfather. He's doing fine. You'll be glad to hear he's back to normal."

Without giving Caroline a chance to say anything, Mei Li started walking away. She heard Caroline's sputter of anger and realized she should feel at least a twinge of guilt for the satisfaction that gave her. But Mei Li didn't.

When she came around the front of Michael's house, he was already waiting for her. It hadn't even been five minutes, and he was changed, wearing a pair of white slacks with a black cotton shirt. He was leaning against his car with his arms folded over his broad chest and his legs crossed at the ankles. He was lost in deep thought, his expression hard and glittering. Again she sensed dangerous ruthlessness, manacled for the moment but very much a part of him.

"I have a brother and for that matter a sister who could take lessons from you on dressing fast," Mei Li said in a light, cheerful voice as she stepped forward.

At first she wasn't sure he had heard her. Then he slowly swung his head toward her, the hard edge in his black eyes vanishing. But still she shivered at that brief expression deep in his eyes. She forced herself to continue in a light tone as she climbed into the passenger's side, "It takes my older sister hours just to pick an outfit to wear."

"I've learned to be quick over the years. It's gotten me out of a few scrapes."

She turned her head toward him. "Just what does a liaison agent for the State Department do?"

"A little bit of everything," he answered quietly, not wanting to elaborate on his job. That part of his life was behind him.

"Top secret?"

"Some." He looked at her. "You'll have to tell me which way to go."

At the end of the driveway Mei Li gave Michael directions to her parents' home, aware as she spoke that the topic of his past job was off limits. She wasn't sure what subject was safe to talk about, but she realized that she wanted to know more about Michael Rutledge.

"Are you here on vacation?" she asked finally.

"Yes. When Kurt told me his house was available, it sounded like the ideal place."

For what? Escape? Mei Li couldn't help but wonder. Michael was running away from something. Did it have to do with the job he wouldn't discuss? "Do you plan to settle down here? Or is this just temporary?"

There was a long pause before Michael replied, "I'm not sure. I have no ties anyplace."

"Not even in Washington, where you lived?"

"Especially not in Washington." His grip on the steering wheel tightened. "I was rarely there."

"I suppose traveling would be fun for some people, but I'm content right here."

"But then, this is paradise." Sarcasm laced his words. "Most people don't live in a place like this."

Mei Li laughed. "It's strange how people call Hawaii paradise. Yes, it's tropical, but the weather can be horrible like any other place. I think paradise is a state of mind. There are people in Hawaii who are unhappy and dissatisfied with their lives. It isn't paradise to them."

Michael glanced at Mei Li, sure she was directing her comment at him. But she was staring straight ahead, her thoughts on someone else. "Who?"

"Am I talking about?"

"Yes."

"My father." She kept her gaze trained on the road ahead.

"Why do you say that?"

"Because my father sees his dream slowly rotting away."

His brow creased. "Rotting away? That's an unusual way of putting something."

61

"His charter boat is rotting right out from under him. Ever since I can remember, his life has been that boat and his family. He needs a new one, or at the very least the one he has needs a major overhaul. Either way it would cost a lot of money that our family doesn't have." She turned toward him, strangely at ease talking to him about her doubts and fears. "Our home used to be filled with such happiness, but now there's a sadness I can't do anything about. Oh, to the outside observer everything appears normal, but I can feel it. It's almost like a time bomb waiting to explode."

"There are ways to raise money. Maybe Lawrence could help."

"No!"

The word was spoken so quickly and vehemently that Michael swerved his gaze to Mei Li. "Why not?"

"My father and Lawrence don't get along."

"Why?" Michael probed, used to delving into people's lives. Being the inquisitor came naturally to him.

"I don't know," she answered, a frantic note in her words. Lately the past seemed to be more important than ever.

When Michael had parked in front of her parents' house, Mei Li faced him, the small confines of the car made their closeness more intimate. She didn't want the evening to end. "Will you come in and meet my parents? There's always room at the table for another person. When you have a large family, someone is often bringing a friend home for dinner."

Michael was about to refuse, but then Mei Li said the word *friend*. It was hard to resist that offer. "Yes, I'd like to," he replied impulsively, a part of him surprised at his acceptance. Mei Li was a woman who demanded more than he could ever give.

"First I should warn you that my nieces and nephews might latch on to you and never let go."

"Nieces and nephews? How many?"

"Oh, I'd say anywhere from one to ten could be here tonight."

"Ten?" One thick eyebrow shot up.

"I told you I have a large family. I won't blame you if you chicken out."

"Put that way, I wouldn't dare. My male ego would never recover from the blow. Surely I can survive ten children for a hour or so."

"Have you been around children much?"

Their gazes locked, the seconds evolving into a full minute. The intimacy heightened with each passing moment until Mei Li felt overwhelmed. The sensual fire in Michael's eyes was banked, but she still could feel its scorching probe.

"No," he replied in a whisper, dispelling the moment of closeness.

Trembling, Mei Li opened her door and stood. Placing her hands on the top of his coupe to still their shaking, she leaned back down to look inside. "Then, Michael Rutledge, you may be eating your words in twenty minutes," she declared with a shaky laugh.

He climbed from his side of the car, and they faced each other over the top of his Mercedes. She felt roped by the captivating tethers of his gaze.

"Are you going to throw me to the lions?" His question was deceptively soft, caressing her across the space that separated them.

"When the water is cold, the best way to get used to it is to dive right in. If you stand on the edge and study the water too long, you may lose your nerve."

Michael threw back his head and laughed, a low, sexy sound. "I'm not an impulsive person, but since I met you, I've done more impulsive things than I ever have in my whole life."

Mei Li began walking toward the front door, tossing over her shoulder, "You could be lucky tonight. There may only be one or two children."

But the second she opened the door to her parents' house, she knew most of the children were there. Michael came up behind her and peered into the mayhem. She felt the heat of his body searing her through her clothes and wondered how in the world she was going to make it through dinner with her inquisitive family. No doubt all eyes would be trained on them, and tomorrow she was going to be asked a hundred questions.

"You still have time to leave before Mother spots you," she whispered over her shoulder.

He leaned down, close to her ear, one hand on her shoulder. "And have you thinking I'm a chicken? No way. I'm in this for better or worse."

"Just remember that in two hours," Mei Li warned over the shouts of the children before stepping into the house.

An older woman, as small as Mei Li but with more obviously oriental features, approached them, laughter in her sparkling black eyes. "We've been expecting you for an hour, daughter." Jade Vandenburg looked closely at Mei Li and asked, "What has happened?"

"There was an accident at Lawrence's house. He fell into the pool."

"He's all right?" her mother asked anxiously.

Wondering about her mother's tone of voice, Mei Li nodded.

Her mother sighed and shifted her attention to Michael.

Mei Li laid her hand on Michael's arm and said, "Mother, this is Michael Rutledge, Lawrence's next-door neighbor. He gave me a lift home since Charlie had to leave. Michael, Jade Vandenburg."

Jade placed her hand in Michael's. "You will stay for dinner?"

"Yes, if it's not too much trouble." He scanned the room filled with people, suddenly feeling trapped by this family scene. His experience was very limited in this area.

"When you cook for this many, one more is no trouble. I'll let Mei Li introduce you to the clan."

Mei Li weaved her fingers through his and entered the living room where everyone was sitting. All eyes turned toward them, and Mei Li went around the room, introducing her family to Michael. He had always been a quick learner, but it took all his concentration to remember who everyone was—all eighteen of them. When the introductions were complete, the family members returned to their conversations.

Mei Li started for her father. Michael began to follow when he felt someone tugging on his pant leg. He looked down into the face of a four-year-old girl with pigtails.

"You're big," Karin said. "My daddy is big, too."

Michael wasn't sure what to say to the little girl. He knelt on his haunches and asked, "Which one is your daddy?"

Karin pointed to the large blond-haired man named Thomas, Mei Li's brother-in-law. "I have a baby brother. Do you want to see him? He's in the crib asleep over there."

Michael couldn't imagine anyone sleeping through this din. "Yes."

Karin took his hand and led him to the crib. Inside was a baby not more than a few months old, sound asleep. Michael was amazed.

"What's your brother's name?"

"Matt. I help take care of him," she said proudly. "I've changed a diaper."

"You have!" Michael wasn't sure he himself could do that successfully. His expertise lay in totally different areas.

"Well, Mommie helped."

"Michael, Dad would like to meet you," Mei Li broke in. "Karin, Grandma is serving the kids dinner now." After her niece ran off toward the backyard, Mei Li said, "We eat in shifts. The kids first. If the weather is good, we eat outside."

Michael watched the exodus of the children. "Who takes care of the kids while the adults are eating?"

"The older ones. The system works pretty well. Occasionally someone has to referee a disagreement, but believe me, you hear about it before it becomes a full-fledged fight," she explained as she walked toward the chair her father was occupying. The man rose as Mei Li made the introductions.

Tall, with blond hair, Charles Vandenburg's appearance was characteristic of his Dutch ancestors, a stark contrast to Jade's petite build and dark coloring. They made a striking couple, Michael thought, comparing them mentally with how he and Mei Li must look together. He quickly dismissed the image from his mind.

"My daughter tells me you live next door to Harris," Charles said. "You're renting the Mc-Neil house?"

"For a couple of months," Michael replied.

"What do you do for a living that you can afford to take a two-month vacation?"

Michael suddenly understood where Mei Li got her candor. "I'm between jobs." He got the distinct impression that he was being interviewed.

"What did you do?"

"Dad, I thought that before we ate I would show Michael my greenhouse," Mei Li cut into the drill.

"Sure. We'll talk later," Charles said. "I need to see what's keeping your brother. Charlie's usually late, but this is really late. Harris has probably dangled another job in his face. Can't that man be satisfied with you working for him?" The animosity in his voice was clear.

"Charlie isn't at Lawrence's, Dad."

Mei Li's father scowled. But before he said another word, the front door opened and Charlie came rushing into the house.

"Sorry, I'm late." When Charlie saw Mei Li, he asked, "Is Mr. Harris all right?"

"Fine," she replied, aware of her father's growing anger.

"You two may work for the man, but you do not have to discuss him in this house."

"He had an accident today. He fell into the pool," Charlie said as an excuse for forgetting that Lawrence Harris wasn't a favorite subject around his father.

"Serves him right," Charles mumbled.

"Come on, Michael, before I'm dragged into the middle of this." Mei Li again took Michael's hand. It was a nice feeling, he realized.

Outside they skirted the part of the yard where the children were eating and headed for the greenhouse at the back of the Vandenburgs' property. The warm tropical air encased them, and the sounds of the children filled the night with merriment.

"Dad built this for me several years ago. He was hoping to entice me to stay home. It didn't work, but I do come here a lot."

"I get the feeling that even if there wasn't a greenhouse, you'd be here a lot."

She stopped at the door and turned to face him. He grasped her other hand and she tilted back her head to gaze up into his dark, penetrating eyes. "Family is important to me. Of course, there are times when they're too interfering, but I've learned to say no. I like my privacy, but I'd be lost without a large family around me."

"Why aren't you married with a horde of kids?"

Her smile lighted her whole face. "It's simple. I haven't found the right man. Why aren't you married?" she countered bluntly.

"I've been too busy. Like a flower, a relationship has to have attention." He had learned that lesson the hard way. He didn't have to go through the pain a second time to realize that women like Mei Li wanted and needed a solid, gently loving relationship, something he could never give her. Even out in the open he felt the walls closing in on him, and he cursed himself for being so damned impulsive in accepting her invitation. She was a symbol of everything he had stayed clear of for so many years.

"Come inside. I have something I want to show you," she said excitedly.

Leave now without an explanation, his common sense demanded.

She pulled him into the greenhouse.

Too late. He heard the cell door slam shut behind him and silently cursed.

She led him down a row of beautiful flowers and plants to the back of the greenhouse, where she stopped and swept her arm wide. "This is my pride and joy."

Before him was every conceivable color and size of orchids. He had seen many of them in their natural state in the Amazon. In the jungle they were parasites, living off the host plants. That was how he had come to view women in general. The flower underlined the growing alarm in his mind.

Mei Li turned toward Michael and immediately sensed his withdrawal. His eyes were piercing as they scanned the orchids. She wanted to reach out and smooth his lined brow, but she dared not. His forbidding look focused on her and sent a shiver down her spine.

"I think I'll decline dinner. Please give my regrets to your parents." His voice was stiffly normal, his eyes effectively masking his emotions.

"No."

He had started to leave, but her denial stopped him. He looked back at Mei Li.

The glint in his eyes would unnerve most people. Intuitively she realized people avoided getting Michael angry, but even that didn't stop her. "You can tell my parents yourself." The strength in her voice surprised her.

He continued to challenge her with his regard. Silence vibrated between them like the frequency of an air-warning signal.

She knew she should heed the warning, but she didn't. "Why do you want to leave?"

He shrugged, but the gesture was filled with tension.

"You are a chicken after all, Michael Rutledge," she half teased, half challenged.

The hardness in his eyes sharpened. "What did you say?"

The menacing calm in his voice chilled her, but she lifted her chin defiantly. Michael reminded her of Lawrence when she had first gone to work for him—brooding, lonely, afraid to feel, to be a part of other people's

72

lives. "You heard me. Chicken," she challenged again.

Michael took a step toward her. A nerve twitched in his jaw.

"Why does my family scare you?" She bravely flung the question at him, but her knees were shaking, and she was having a difficult time standing her ground. Yet this was too important for her to back away. She wanted to know the answer to that question and many more she had concerning Michael Rutledge.

Silence.

"Chicken," she murmured, slicing through the disconcerting silence, provoking him as she never had another human being—not even Lawrence.

His hands clenched at his sides as he closed the distance between them. Mei Li pressed herself against the counter, her hands gripping its edge to steady herself.

"You're brave, Mei Li," he muttered in a deceptively soft tone. His quiet voice was more frightening than if he had shouted at her.

"Candid, which is more than you're being with me and possibly yourself," she replied daring him once more with her words. "If you were truthful—"

"Truthful? There are many kinds of truths."

73

His face was dangerously close, and his warm breath fanned her cheek. His body blocked any escape; his arms on either side of her pinned her against him. She didn't know why she was pushing him into a corner, but she sensed he hadn't felt intensely in a very long time, that he had locked his emotions inside with a control most people could never have. She wanted to unleash those emotions and make him truly feel again.

"Why do you want to leave? Why are you running?" She taunted him with her calmly spoken questions. Even his anger was better than nothing.

His hands snaked up to grasp her arms and pull her against his solid strength. "Feeling reckless?" His words held his own taunt.

She tilted her head back. "You haven't answered my question," she demanded in a level voice.

The curve of her mouth, inches away from his, mocked him with her unruffled serenity. Her jasmine scent wafted to him as the alarm signals grew louder in his mind. He glared down at her, trying to dismiss the seductive feel of her body against his, the power this woman had to incite emotions in him that he had thought were buried.

"Chicken," she whispered.

His mouth covered hers forcefully. His fin-

74

gers dug into her upper arms as he forced her lips apart, his tongue sweeping boldly into her mouth to claim its sweetness. His invading tongue thrust in and out while his arms closed about her, squeezing the breath from her.

Stunned by the savagery of his kiss, she went limp in his arms. She had goaded him into this. She was shocked as much at her behavior as at his. His turbulent intensity passed right through her.

For a few seconds nothing registered in Michael's mind except his anger, his need to wash her scent and feel from his thoughts. Then slowly he realized her nonresistance, and he shoved himself away, disgusted at his lack of control, at the fact that he had let her get to him as no one had since Laura. He turned his back on her, fighting for control.

"You haven't answered my question."

Her quiet words prodded him again, but this time he had control. "After the last few minutes I didn't think I had to answer. You're a smart lady. Figure it out for yourself."

"No. I want you to spell it out for me."

He whirled to face her, hauling her back into his embrace, his fist clutching her hair, yanking her head back until their gazes clashed. "Stubborn bitch." He was sure no one had ever called her that, and her shocked look confirmed his suspicion. "You're dangerous to be around."

Her eyes widened. "Dangerous? Me?"

"Don't play innocent with me. You can't stand there with your body thrust against mine like this and expect me to believe it." She was too beautiful not to know her effect on men, not to have experienced firsthand the result when a man gazed into her alluring black eyes and held her in his arms.

"I am thrust, as you say, against you because you're holding me tightly—painfully hard, I might add."

The innate dignity in her voice touched a protected cord inside him. He had to get away from her before she had him believing in her, thinking there was a possible chance for them. He drew within himself, all traces of emotion wiped from his face.

Releasing her and stepping away, he said in a cool, impersonal voice, "This is all wrong for me. It's not my scene. Tell your parents whatever you wish. I'm leaving now."

And before Mei Li could say another word, he was gone. Her fingertips grazed her bruised lips, and she thought it was for the best that he had left. But for a few seconds he had reacted with intense emotions. What would it be like if he totally let himself go, to feel again? She wasn't sure it would be wise to find out.

CHAPTER FOUR

Mei Li lifted her hand to knock, then hesitated. Dropping her hand back to her side, she started to leave, but the sounds of the *Romeo and Juliet* overture halted her. She listened for a moment to the music, then determinedly turned back and pounded on Michael's sliding-glass door.

The door was wrenched open, and the passageway was filled with Michael's large, menacing frame. He scowled down at her silently.

For a long, tense moment Mei Li was transfixed by his imposing figure, towering in front of her like an avenging god. His sun-streaked hair was unruly, as if he had repeatedly run his fingers through it. His face was unshaven, leaving a dark sinister cast to his features. He was dressed only in a pair of white shorts, revealing the toughened planes of his body and his powerful legs. A fine white scar that ran across his shoulder stood out against his tanned skin. But what arrested Mei Li the most was the way Michael's ebony eyes glittered with some sort of demands.

She shivered in the warmth of the late morning sun and thrust the pot she held toward him. "A peace offering," she murmured through parched lips as she stared up into his brooding eyes.

A nerve quivered in his firmly set jaw. As his intimidating gaze moved to the orchid plant, the music thundered to a finish; then silence filled the house. Still he remained quiet.

"I shouldn't have said those things to you last night," Mei Li continued, wishing he would say something—anything!

"Why did you come here?" he demanded finally. The harsh line of his stubbled jaw strengthened.

"Because I don't like the way things were left between us. And because Lawrence is expecting you for lunch, and I didn't think you'd show up since I was going to be there, too."

He stepped back, intending to shut the door. Mei Li stepped boldly forward, one part of her marveling at her bravery. Mei Li had had to bully her way into Lawrence's life, but she had eventually won his trust and friendship. She was resolved to do the same with Michael.

"This orchid requires sunlight, and it should be watered when the soil gets dry. They aren't hard to raise."

She entered the house, scanning the living room for a place to set the plant. When she saw a table in front of a window, she put the pot on it, then faced Michael, outwardly calm, inwardly shaking at the picture he made standing in the middle of the room with his feet braced apart and his hands on his hips. He appeared every inch a man capable of taking care of himself in dangerous situations. She must be crazy to push this man, she thought.

"You know, most people think orchids are parasites. They aren't. They only anchor to the host plant; they don't draw nourishment from it."

A nerve in his jaw twitched again. He remembered comparing Mei Li to an orchid. Even if an orchid wasn't a parasite, it was still a valid comparison. An orchid was extremely close to its host plant, something he hadn't been to another person since his parents' death. That was one of the reasons his marriage to Laura had failed.

"Orchids will make this place . . ." Her voice faded under his intense regard. She swallowed and added, "You will come, won't

79

you? Lawrence wants to thank you properly." Her voice cracked, and she swallowed again.

His penetrating dark eyes continued their scrutiny, and she had to resist the urge to shiver. He would notice any movement on her part, and she didn't want him to know how deeply he affected her. He was always keenly alert, watching, waiting, assessing.

"I don't need to be thanked. It was nothing."

"Please come."

When she turned her large pleading eyes on him, something snapped inside him. The taut strain that had gripped him since the night before flowed from his body. His hands fell to his sides, and he relaxed the stiff set of his shoulders. He was so damned tired of fighting himself.

"Fine," he clipped out, realizing in one part of his mind that he was again doing something he knew he shouldn't.

Her face brightened. "Good. Lawrence had the cook prepare something special for you."

He rubbed his hand over his stubble, wishing he weren't so damned confused about Mei Li. "It'll be a few minutes."

"I'll wait." She wasn't going to leave and give him a chance to change his mind.

Michael started to say something but instead shrugged and left the room.

Mei Li looked about her. She had been in Kurt McNeil's house before with Lawrence. There were only a few personal items of Michael's; otherwise, everything was Kurt's. There was a collection of classical music sitting on the cabinet where the stereo was. That had to be Michael's—Kurt was a country-western fan. There was a book about Hawaii opened on the coffee table, and next to the book a watch that she had seen Michael wear. Those were the only things that indicated he lived in the house. She sensed that to the places he had been he had brought little of himself and that he had left nothing behind when he departed. Suddenly she wondered if he would leave the orchid there when he left Hawaii.

"Ready."

Startled from her thoughts, she spun to find Michael only a few feet behind her. She hadn't even heard him approach. He was a man of the night—silent, dark, brooding.

All her senses were centered on his masculine power. His heady male scent, the element of danger and mystery that surrounded him, and his roughly hewn features all combined to form a picture of strength and force that overwhelmed Mei Li each time she was in his presence.

"I didn't hear you come in," she murmured, not sure what to say.

He gave her a look that said she wasn't supposed to. "It's almost twelve, and I believe Lawrence likes to begin on time."

"He would even if we weren't there," Mei Li said with a laugh, trying to ignore his cool tone. "Once I was late for lunch because I lost track of the time in the garden. He was having dessert when I showed up twenty minutes late."

"Do you have lunch with him often?"

Mei Li glanced at Michael as they left his house, trying to discern what was behind his question. She could tell nothing from his voice or expression.

"About once a month," she replied.

"Your relationship with Lawrence Harris is more than employer and employee."

It wasn't a question, and Mei Li bristled. She stopped and said in a frosty voice, "If you mean we are friends, yes. If you mean more than that, go to hell, Michael Rutledge." John Harris inferring that was one thing, but coming from Michael it hurt—more than she wanted to acknowledge. Mei Li stormed past him, deciding this was one stray dog that could bite, and she would be better off leaving him alone.

His fingers clasped around her upper arm

82

and pulled her back around, close to him—dangerously close. "Why would I think you were anything but friends? You don't give me much credit for observation, lady. Anyone can see the bond between you two."

She pointedly looked down at his hand gripping her arm, then back up into his dark eyes. "Then why did you say it?"

"I was making an observation. Why are you so defensive?"

Using his disarming technique of silence, she took a moment to compose an answer. She realized the reason she had reacted so intensely was because she didn't want Michael to have the wrong impression of her relationship with Lawrence. Usually she didn't care what people thought but she discovered that she cared what Michael thought. "Because Lawrence's son thinks I'm after his father's money."

The hardness in his eyes softened, and his hand eased its grasp. Michael massaged her arm where his fingers had dug into her flesh, his caress in opposition to his bruising grip. "His son is a fool."

"Why do you say that?" Her question was a rush of breathless words, because his seductive touch was doing strange things to her.

"Anyone can see that the bond of friendship between you and Lawrence is genuine."

His head dipped toward hers, their eyes bound in a sensual link.

Mei Li's heartbeat pounded like the surf, and her throat tightened.

His mouth was inches from hers; his warm breath tickled her lips. Mei Li pressed her body against his as her eyelids closed.

Suddenly he pulled back, ran his hand down her arm once more, and released her. "We don't want to keep Lawrence waiting."

"No, we don't," she murmured in disappointment, feeling as if she had been on a roller coaster with Michael and was still light-headed from the ride.

Lawrence was on the terrace when they mounted the stairs to the house. The table was set for three, which was a relief to Mei Li. She didn't think she could sit through a lunch with a member of Lawrence's family, too. With Michael she already felt her emotions had been pulled in a hundred different directions. She was doing and feeling things she had never done and felt before. Her life had always been on an even keel until now.

"So good to see you again," Lawrence said, shaking Michael's hand.

"You're looking much better, Mr. Harris."

"Lawrence, please. After all, you saved my life."

Lawrence turned to Mei Li, a twinkle in his

blue eyes. "Don't the Chinese have a saying that if you save a person's life you're responsible for that person?"

"Yes, you know very well they do," she answered, a smile touching the corners of her mouth. Her uncle and Lawrence had sat up many nights talking about their heritages and customs.

Michael frowned as he took a seat at the table. "It wasn't anything that dramatic."

"Nonsense, my boy. I'm sitting here because of you."

Mei Li sensed that the last thing Michael Rutledge wanted at this time was to be responsible for someone else. Again she felt the loneliness of his life and wondered why he was so determined to stand apart.

"Speaking of the accident, have you had someone look at the brakes on the wheelchair?" Michael asked casually.

"No, I had Mrs. Duncan give it away. This is a new one. I have no patience to wait for it to be fixed. Besides, it was two years old. Time for a newer model." Lawrence's eyes danced merrily.

"Is it still here?"

"No, I'm sure Mrs. Duncan took it away this morning."

"Where?" Michael leaned forward, alert.

"I don't know. Her husband probably took

it to the Oahu Mission. But why all these questions?"

Sitting back in his chair again, Michael shrugged. "I'm just naturally a suspicious guy. It seems strange that your brakes failed at that particular moment. I'm sure it's nothing to be alarmed about, though."

"You think someone tried to kill me?" Lawrence asked, his features ashening.

Mei Li couldn't believe the direction the conversation was taking. Like Lawrence, her full attention was on Michael.

"No, I didn't say that. It's just a possibility—a remote one, I'm sure."

Lawrence thought a minute. "I suppose I could try to track down the wheelchair and have it checked to be on the safe side."

"It wouldn't hurt. I believe in checking all possibilities out."

"Part of your former job?" Mei Li interjected, realizing that if she knew about what he used to do, she might understand him better.

"You could say that," Michael replied tersely, dismissing the subject with his tone of voice.

When the maid brought the lunch out to the terrace, Lawrence turned the conversation to light, amusing anecdotes of his budding career in Hawaii during the late forties.

He had been stationed at Pearl Harbor during World War II and had fallen in love with the islands. When he had left the navy, this island had been the place he had decided to make his home.

"Of course, at that time it was a lot different," Lawrence said between bites of Macadamian Chicken, a dish of boneless chicken breasts fried in a light batter, smothered in a sweet and sour sauce, then sprinkled with chopped macadamia nuts. "My granddaughter would say I'm one of the reasons that Hawaii's face has changed so much in forty years. But if it hadn't been me, it would have been someone else. At least I've tried to preserve the beauty and essence of the islands."

"Granddaddy, isn't that what Hitler said after conquering Europe? If it hadn't been me, it would have been someone else. At least I tried to wipe out a whole culture." Caroline, clad in cutoff jeans and a bikini bra, appeared on the terrace, a beach bag clutched in her hand.

"Eavesdropping again?" Lawrence asked sarcastically, not even looking in his granddaughter's direction.

"I find out such interesting things that way." Caroline came around to stand in front of Lawrence and next to Michael. She rested a hand on the back of Michael's chair, her lips pulled down in a pout. "I had the best of intentions when I came out here."

"Oh?" One side of Lawrence's mouth quirked as if to say he doubted it.

"I wanted to know if you were all right today. I didn't realize you were having a"—Caroline's gaze skimmed over her grandfather and Mei Li to fasten on Michael—" a party. If I had known, I could have changed my plans and joined you." One perfectly manicured fingertip slid back and forth along Michael's chair.

Mei Li gripped the arms of her chair.

She had never been jealous in her whole life; this was a new sensation, and Mei Li didn't like it one bit. In fact, lately she had been feeling a lot of new sensations where Michael was concerned. She focused her energies inward and took deep breaths to compose herself.

"Well, don't let us keep you from your other plans. No doubt you're preserving the heritage of surfing."

Mei Li found herself silently applauding Lawrence's reply.

Caroline, her features contorted in anger, shot back, "It's part of the Hawaiian culture."

"Is that the reason you devote seven days a week to it? Maybe I should cut off your allowance—which I might add was only made possible by *raping* these islands. Maybe it's about time you got a job." Lawrence slammed his hand on the arm of his wheelchair. "Sometimes I'm a little slow on what to do about my family, but I've just realized I'm not doing you any favors by paying your way in this world. Get a job, or there will be no more money from me."

"You wouldn't," Caroline sputtered.

"I would."

Caroline glared at her grandfather for a full minute before stomping back into the house.

"I'm sorry about that, Mei Li, Michael. It's been coming for quite some time and once I got going I couldn't stop myself," Lawrence announced, then picked up his fork to finish his meal.

But as they ate in silence, Mei Li noticed that Lawrence hardly touched the rest of his food. He cared more for his family than they cared for him. Maybe by cutting Caroline loose he would be doing the right thing, Mei Li thought. But remembering that last look Caroline had leveled at him, Mei Li wasn't so sure. She had never seen such a display of anger and . . . well, hatred.

For dessert the maid served them slices of coconut cream pie. Mei Li sought to lighten the mood by talking about the antics of her nieces and nephews. She was acutely aware, however, of Michael's growing, moody silence. By the time lunch was over he hadn't contributed to the conversation in fifteen minutes.

Lawrence relaxed back in his wheelchair, sipping his herbal tea. "Have you had a chance to see my garden, Michael?"

"Briefly."

"I wish I could give you a tour. I'm proud of Mei Li's accomplishments. You should have seen these grounds before she came." He sighed heavily, but the gleam of mischief was back in his blue eyes. "Alas, yesterday took more out of me than I thought. Of course, Mei Li would be the best guide you could have, anyway."

"I'm sure she would, but—"

"I'd be glad to show you my creation," Mei Li broke in, realizing by the set of Michael's jaw that he was about to refuse the tour. She rose, challenging him with her look.

The strong slope of his jaw clenched into a firm line. Without a word he pushed back his chair and stood, his large frame dwarfing her.

Mei Li hurried from the terrace. She didn't have to glance back to know that Lawrence was smiling with satisfaction and that Michael was glaring at her.

She paused beneath a white plumeria tree, its sweet fragrance drifted to her, and she waited for Michael. As he walked toward her, the harsh slant of his mouth indicated his displeasure at her manipulation.

"Ready?" She asked cheerfully.

"No. I have things to do this afternoon. I'll have to take a rain check on the tour."

"What things?" she inquired boldly, amazed at her continual audacity.

His eyes narrowed on her. He stepped even closer. "I'm expecting a phone call in an hour."

"Good. I'll give you the quick tour." She started forward.

As she passed him, his hand caught her wrist. "Mei Li, it won't work."

"What won't work?"

"Us."

"Us?" She tilted her head to one side and looked at him.

"I'm forty, twice your age."

"I'm twenty-three. My birthday is in a few months. Besides, what does age have to do with anything?"

"Different generations, different expectations."

"I still don't see why we can't be friends," she said, the challenge back in her voice.

"That's all you expect?" One eyebrow rose mockingly.

"What do you expect?"

He laughed humorlessly. "What's been between us has nothing to do with friendship, Mei Li. You and I both know that."

"What are you afraid of? Feeling?" Please open up, she pleaded with her eyes.

"Yes, damn it!" His grip on her wrist tightened. He was unnerved by the look in her wide eyes.

"Why? It's normal for people."

"I haven't lived a normal life."

"Because of your job?"

"Partly."

"What's the other part?"

"I thought you were going to give me a quick tour."

Her eyes drilled into him. She wished she could tell what was behind his unreadable expression. She wished she could reach him. Patience, Chang would counsel, and she realized that with Michael she would have to have a great deal of it.

"Let's start with these bird of paradise plants." She gestured toward the brilliant orange petals with dark blue stamens; the flowers were in the shape of a bird's head.

Throughout the tour Michael listened attentively but without comment. At the end they stopped in the shaded forest terrain of Lawrence's property near the beach. A vine with white flowers hung from the tree near them.

"What are those?" Michael asked, wanting to keep their conversation on the subject of flowers, yet realizing it would be so easy not to. Around Mei Li he seemed to lack the control he usually had.

Mei Li blushed. "Passion flowers. Their fruit is used in juices and jellies." When Mei Li glanced in Michael's direction, he had moved nearer to her.

"There's so much beauty in this garden that a person could begin to take it for granted if he weren't careful. I haven't thanked you for the orchid you brought me earlier." His voice dropped to a husky level.

"I have plenty to share."

"Yes, you would know how to share."

"With three sisters and two brothers it's a necessity."

"That's just the point. I don't have any family. I grew up an only child. In everything you do you share yourself."

"Is that why my family scared you off last night?" She took a step toward him, trying to bridge the distance physically as well as emotionally.

"No." He massaged the nape of his neck in frustration. "Yes. The truth is I've had no experience when it comes to large families."

"I can understand that. You're a private man. Even to me they're a little overwhelming at times. But I wouldn't know what to do without them and their love."

He looked away. "Ever since I can remember I've had to keep everything inside. Why is it so easy for you to express yourself?"

"If you want to have any kind of an identity as an individual in a large family, you have to express your feelings, or you get swallowed up by the whole."

He continued to stare at the garden that Mei Li had so tenderly created. "Lawrence is right. You've done a wonderful job here. Have you always wanted to be a gardener?" He turned around to snare her gaze with his.

"My uncle taught me everything he knows about gardening. He's been retired for five years, but at one time he was the best on the island."

"But is it what you wanted?"

"It's where I escape to be myself," she stated candidly. "This is me." She swept her arm out to indicate the garden. "It is an expression of my individuality. To me this garden is like an artist's canvas. I believe that to be whole a person needs a way to express his creativity."

Michael glanced down at his watch. "I should go, or I'll miss that call."

"I'll walk with you to the garden's edge."

"You don't have to," he said immediately.

"I want to," she countered, falling in step beside him on the stone path. She got the distinct impression that if she didn't make the next move, Michael wouldn't, either.

At the hibiscus hedge, Michael paused to say good-bye. "I enjoyed the tour."

"You never did see all of my greenhouse. Tonight I promise only my parents and one sister are going to be at the house. Come to dinner, please."

"Are you always this persistent?"

"When it matters."

"Why does it matter?"

"I don't know. It just does." Bravely she reached out and took his hand. "Please come. It will be tame compared to last night."

His first instinct was to draw her to him; his second was to push her away and escape. Instead, he picked a red hibiscus and placed it in her hair.

"It's hard to say no to you." His hands framed her face.

"Then that means you'll come?"

He couldn't resist the smile in her almond-shaped eyes. "Yes, I'll come."

"And stay to the end?" She covered his hands with hers.

"And stay until you're ready to leave." He

leaned forward and brushed his lips across hers. He had wanted to do that for a long time.

Mei Li melted against him; her arms wound around his neck as his tongue invaded her honeyed cavity. The tip of his tongue ran over her smooth, white teeth, then flicked the corners of her mouth before he trailed tiny kisses to her earlobe. She clung to him as his tongue circled the shell of her ear, sending tingling quivers through her body.

"Damn, why did you come into my life?" he whispered.

Shaken with unfamiliar sensations and puzzled by his words, she arched slightly away from him.

He again trapped her head between his large hands. He looked long and hard into her eyes. "I don't want to hurt you."

"You won't."

He pulled away. "Hell, Mei Li, you're too trusting." Then he disappeared through the hibiscus hedge.

CHAPTER FIVE

Mei Li caught up with Michael halfway across his yard. "And you don't trust at all."

Her softly spoken words halted him in mid-stride. He kept his back to her as he replied, "That ability was taken away from me a long time ago."

"How, Michael?" She moved around to stand in front of him, her expression determined. "Trust me, Michael. You have to start somewhere."

His black, piercing gaze bored into hers. The hardened twist to his jawline spoke of the battle raging within him. "You have no idea the kind of life I've led."

"No, I don't. But I'm a good listener." She needed to understand.

"Betrayal, intrigue, danger, and for that matter death have been common elements in my life for years. There have been many times when I've gone into a situation and not been able to trust a soul. And you ask me to trust you? I don't know how to, Mei Li."

The intensity in his voice shook her, but she remained calm and said in a gently flowing voice, "We start by getting to know each other. Trust comes from knowing another person well."

His laughter held no humor. "I know you well enough, or rather your kind."

"And what kind is that?"

"Your type wants marriage and a home with children. Your type wants all of a man."

"I won't deny that isn't something I want. But right now all I'm asking for is a chance for us to get to know each other. That's all."

"No, lady, you want much more."

"You can't keep running the rest of your life. You're going to have to stop sometime. Why not now?"

His gaze swerved away from hers. "You're already demanding more of me than anyone has in a long time."

"Maybe something inside of you is telling you this is the time to stop. Maybe it's about time that someone demanded of you."

His gaze veered back to her face. "I can promise you nothing, Mei Li."

"I'm not asking for promises."

His look told her he didn't quite believe her.

"You'll still come to dinner at my parents'?"

"No."

She started to protest when he laid his finger over her lips. "I'd rather we have dinner at my house. I'll cook. After all, how can we get to know each other with so many people around?"

His finger lingered on her mouth, rubbing across it. Her heartbeat began to do triple time while her eyelids half closed. He slipped his hand around to the nape of her neck and drew her to him, his lips feathering across hers once, then twice.

As he ran his fingers through her hair, the hibiscus fluttered to the ground. One hand pressed her into his hard body while the other held her head still. His mouth ravished hers, his teeth nipping gently at her lower lip between kisses.

Her arms closed around him as her head tipped back, and he kissed the white column of her neck. His tongue flicked in and out of the hollow at the base of her throat, spurring her pulse even faster. She clutched at him to steady herself before she completely collapsed from the exhilarating sensations he was producing in her.

"I don't like how I lose control around you," he murmured against the sensitive flesh of her neck.

His words seemed to sober him because he set her away with a firm resolution. Yet there was no anger in his expression, only confusion. He shook his head, massaging the back of his neck.

"Do you still want me to come to dinner?" she asked, praying he wouldn't withdraw again.

"Yes," Michael answered, moving past her. At the door into his house, he called back, "At seven."

When Michael opened the door at seven that evening, Mei Li smiled, placed a lei around his neck, and kissed his cheek chastely, saying, "Aloha, Michael." Then she walked into the house.

She turned around in the center of the living room to face him. "I started to bring you another orchid, then decided I'd better see how you manage with the first one. So instead, I made you a lei. I bet when you arrived you didn't get one, and no one should come to the islands without receiving the traditional greeting."

She knew she was chattering nervously, but the desirous look in Michael's eyes was melting her insides. Though she didn't have much experience when it came to men, she knew that what was between them was explosive, capable of rocking her very core.

"It will keep for days in the refrigerator," she continued, nervously, lacing her fingers together in front of her.

His gaze slowly traveled down her, taking in her red and black silk dress with its mandarin collar and short-capped sleeves. The long dress had a slit in each side up to her thighs, exposing her slender legs and delicate ankles. Her hair hung loose and down her back nearly to her waist. She wore a red hibiscus in her jet-black hair like the one he had given her earlier that day.

When his gaze reestablished eye contact with hers, she drew in a sharp breath at the fire that flared in his dark eyes. She felt hot even though an ocean breeze cooled the room.

Staring at the vision of beauty before him, he felt his defenses go up. Friends? He laughed silently at that word. Warily he closed the door behind him and walked into the living room.

"Anything to drink?" he offered while fixing himself a Scotch and water.

"Do you have any pineapple juice?"

"No, all I have is orange juice."

"That will be fine," she said, realizing they

sounded like two strangers meeting for the first time.

After handing her the juice, he announced, "Dinner won't be ready for a while. Let's sit out on the deck." Where he could hopefully keep his hands off her, he added silently.

Outside the breeze cooled her flushed cheeks and the orange juice relieved the dryness in her throat. While sipping her drink, she watched Michael over the rim of her glass. Sitting across from her, he was studying her, too, his eyes hooded, veiling his expression. The sky grew dark, and yet neither one spoke.

Finally, when her tattered nerves could no longer take the silence, Mei Li said, "Lawrence wanted me to tell you he tried tracking down the wheelchair, but it isn't where Mr. Duncan took it this morning. He gave it to the Oahu Mission, and they've already given it away."

"Don't they keep records?" Michael tossed down the rest of his drink.

"Apparently not very good ones."

"Awfully convenient if you ask me," he said sardonically.

"Do you always suspect everything?"

"Yes, Mei Li. I tried to tell you that earlier today."

"The Oahu Mission has never worried about red tape. Its only concern is the needy."

"The end result is that the wheelchair has disappeared without being checked."

"So you're convinced someone is trying to kill Lawrence?"

"I didn't say that."

"No, that's right. It's just a possibility."

"Yes, it is."

"Murder!" she said incredulously, shaking her head, trying to digest the implications of what Michael was saying.

"It's not that unusual."

"Maybe not to you, but to me it is."

"You read about it all the time in the paper."

"That's entirely different from knowing someone who was murdered—or almost murdered, as you say. It's hard for me to comprehend."

"And it's not hard for me," he shot back, rising abruptly and standing at the railing.

Mei Lei rose and moved to his side, staring out at the ocean. She felt the tension emanating from him.

"I like this side of the island better than the south," she said, seeking to change the subject. "It's quieter, more peaceful, and away from the tourists that cram Honolulu. I think that's why Lawrence didn't build in Diamond

Head. It's too near the city. Of course, John hates having to commute into Honolulu. The traffic at rush hour is horrible."

Her soft, melodic voice washed over him in soothing waves. He listened to her talk about the island, but her words didn't register, just the inflection of her voice, her calm cadence as she spoke. He gazed at the sun as it rapidly set. The clouds on the horizon were bathed in liquid gold. This was peace, Michael thought as his body slowly relaxed.

"Tomorrow is the Fourth. We always have a big family bash at the beach; then we go to an art fair and fireworks display afterward. I wish you would join us." Mei Li angled her head to the side and looked at his hard profile. He continued to stare out to sea, and she wondered if he had even heard her. "It's always a lot of fun, with plenty of friendly competition and food. Will you come, Michael?"

He turned toward her. His forefinger and thumb lifted her chin so he could stare down into her beautiful, serene face. His thumb caressed her lips, effectively stopping her flow of words. He gathered her to him and held her close against his heart.

For the first time in a very long while he felt at peace with the world, with himself. He clung to that feeling as he clung to Mei Li, for he knew it was fleeting. There were too many demons hounding him to make the serenity last.

"You make it damned hard to refuse you, Mei Li. Yes, I'll join your family for the Fourth —that is, if I'm not intruding on a family affair."

"Are you kidding? Our Fourth of July celebration gets larger every year, and it's not because of the babies. Before long it will become a tourist attraction."

"Then I'll be there. What time and where?"

"I'll pick you up."

His soft chuckle rumbled deep in his chest. "You don't trust me to show up?"

"Truthfully, I'm not sure what you'll do from one minute to the next. But that's not the reason. The beach is off the beaten track. Since you're new to the island, it's easier if I pick you up. I'll be here at nine. We start early."

His embrace tightened around Mei Li. She listened to the pounding of Michael's heart, and she savored the closeness. Something special passed between them in that moment that she couldn't put a name to, but it gave her hope.

"If I don't see about dinner, it will be ruined," he whispered against the top of her head. He squeezed her briefly, then stepped back.

"Can I help?"

"You create in your garden. I create in the kitchen."

"You cook a lot?"

He chuckled. "Don't sound so shocked. Yes, I cook when I get the chance. In fact, I suppose it's my way to express my creativity. I started out wanting to learn the basics because I was getting sick and tired of restaurant food. Eventually I began to experiment and found I enjoyed cooking. But I have to admit that until I came to Hawaii, I didn't find much time to cook."

"I must confess my mother is a good cook, but I've never learned the skill from her. There was always someone older to cook, and I was always busy in the garden."

"Maybe we could swap knowledge someday. I'll be back in a few minutes, I thought we would eat out here on the deck."

As Michael left, Mei Li noticed for the first time that the table was set. The sun was completely down, and the dark shadows of night were closing in. She turned back toward the ocean and relished the salt-scented breeze, the hypnotizing sound of the waves crashing against the shore.

When strong arms circled her and brought her back against solid strength, she didn't resist. It felt so right to be in Michael's embrace with his chest pressed into her back, his arms forming a protective ring around her.

"Dinner is ready," he murmured against her ear.

She turned within the loose band of his arms and glanced at the table. He had lit the lantern on it, casting the china and crystal in a golden sheen. Covered dishes of food were sitting on the table.

"I didn't hear you."

He smiled crookedly. "A habit of mine." He brushed the back of his hand along her jaw. An incredibly tender look was in his eyes. "I hope you're hungry."

His intense regard left her speechless. She nodded once, unable to look away.

"Good. I fixed enough for four." Reluctantly he released her and moved to the table, pulling out a chair for her.

She grasped the railing behind her to steady herself. The passion in his eyes totally unnerved her. She decided that before this evening she hadn't known what it meant to be possessed by a look. As she walked the short distance to the table and sat down, he watched her every move with that penetrating intensity she had come to expect from him.

Leaning down, he breathed deeply of her

jasmine scent. "After we finish with this, I have a dessert, too."

She turned her head to the side; their mouths were inches apart. She started to say something, but his disarming closeness robbed her of all thoughts. Instead, she found herself anticipating his kiss, wanting it desperately.

His mouth sought hers hungrily as his hand came up to hold her head still. The force of his mouth drove into hers with savage conquest in mind, and she surrendered in heart and soul. Burning desire welled up in her and threatened to consume her.

She started to put her arms around his neck when Michael straightened and drew in a ragged breath. "I didn't mean to start with dessert first."

"Not a good idea. It can ruin your appetite for the rest of the meal." She wasn't sure she could eat a thing; her stomach was churning with frustrated desire.

Seated next to her, he lifted the covers on the dishes to reveal a pork crown roast with a mustard-glaze melange, stuffed mushrooms, and poppyseed onion rolls. Their aroma mingled with the scent of flowers and sea in the moisture-laden air to form a mixture of enticing smells.

Mei Li started with the marinated seafood

wraps. Michael waited expectantly while she tasted it.

"Well?" he prompted when she didn't say anything.

"Fishing for a compliment?" she asked with a smile.

"Yes. All artists need them to survive."

"Okay, let me see." She paused for dramatic effect. "The bouquet is delicate, the body light."

His brow wrinkled. "What are you talking about? The wine?"

"Oh, those aren't the right words to use to describe food?" she queried innocently.

"Not in my book."

"Well then, all I can say is, this is great! I'm afraid my mother is going to have to watch out. I think you could become my favorite cook."

"It's just something I threw together." He waved his hand nonchalantly in the air as if his masterpiece had only taken five minutes to prepare.

"Oh, between the sunset and darkness?"

"No, more like between when I left you this afternoon and darkness."

"Six hours?"

"I wanted this to be perfect."

The sensuous look he gave her almost made

her drop her fork. Her pulse raced with a fiery speed through her body.

"Why?" she asked in a quavering voice.

"To impress you."

"We both know you aren't a man who feels he has to impress someone. A person has to take you or leave you the way you are."

He arched one eyebrow in a silent taunt. "And just how am I?"

"I suspect you play by your own rules—which don't necessarily conform to society's." She finished her appetizer and waited as Michael served the main course of pork roast and the assorted vegetables.

"A good part of my life has been spent in the jungle where there's no society to speak of, at least not in civilization's terms, and where there are no rules but nature's."

"The strongest survive?"

"Right." His intense gaze captured hers in the lamplight. "Have you ever killed someone?"

She gasped.

"Of course not. Mei Li, I have. Do you still want to sit here and eat dinner with me?" His question mocked her innocence, her trusting nature.

"Why do you feel the need to frighten me? Every time we talk, the subject of our conversation turns to violence."

He slammed his fist down on the table, sloshing the wine onto the white tablecloth. Mei Li jumped, her eyes riveted to the blood-red spot on the linen.

"Because, damn it, that is the way my life has been up until now." His voice was low and menacing. "I wanted this evening to be perfect because I want to put all that behind me, start fresh with a clean slate. I can't, though. It's there—always."

She wasn't sure what to say. The kind of life he had led was totally alien to her.

"In the course of my work, I've had to kill or be killed. Contrary to popular belief, it doesn't become easier. Each time I felt a part of me die, too. In order to protect my sanity, I shut myself off from other people, from caring about anyone or anything too much. It enabled me to survive." The hollow ring to his voice spoke of the harsh toll his job had exacted on him.

"And now you find yourself in a completely different environment where those rules don't apply?"

"I would like to hope I've left the violent, dark side of my life behind me."

"But you're not sure?"

"No. Just pick up the newspaper and read the front page." He thought of his nagging suspicion concerning Lawrence, and he knew his distrustful, wary side was firmly in place. Gesturing toward her plate, he asked, "Have you had enough?"

She glanced down at her half-eaten dinner and nodded.

He stood and pulled her to her feet. "Let's go for a walk."

Michael took Mei Li's hand and led her toward the beach. They slipped their shoes off and left them by the path. Moonlight streamed across the water, illuminating their way as they headed toward the ocean. The rhythmic sound of the waves and the tranquil darkness of night were in complete contrast to their swirling thoughts.

"How did you ever get into the spy business in the first place?" Mei Li looked up into his shadowed face and could see his jaw clench.

"I was good at what I did. Technically, though, I wasn't in the spy business. I have a doctorate in political affairs and went to work for the State Department after graduation. Coupled with my experience in Vietnam, one thing led to another, and before I realized it I was involved in 'delicate' situations."

"What made you quit?"

His fingers around her tightened. She was probing into explosive territory. "Nothing of importance."

By his tone she knew it was of great importance, but she didn't push. Trust came gradually, and without his trust there could be nothing between them—not even friendship. But she realized in that blinding instant that she wanted much more than friendship from Michael Rutledge.

They walked hand in hand past Lawrence's house, the waves breaking over their feet. The night was a healing balm, meant to wash away cares and concerns as the waves washed away the sand.

Michael stopped, looked up at the star-studded sky, and inhaled deeply. "I never took the time to simply enjoy the ocean. I can understand why people are lured to the sea. There's something very soothing about it."

"Is that why you came to Hawaii, to Kurt's beach house?" Mei Li stood in front of Michael, watching carefully the play of silvery light over his features.

"I hadn't thought so, but perhaps."

"Why are you seeking peace?"

"Doesn't everyone?"

"Not always consciously."

He gazed down into her face, hidden by the night darkness. "I've had very little of it in my life."

He brought his hands up to take her face within them. The potent eloquence of the moment drew her to him, and she placed her hands on his shoulders. His thumb rubbed a gentle circle over her skin while they stared at each other, mesmerized.

"You know, we never did have dessert," he whispered. His words could barely be heard in Mei Li's ears over the pounding of the surf and the thundering of her heartbeat.

"Yes, we did. Remember? We had it first."

"No, that just whetted my appetite for this." Dipping his head toward hers, he kissed her, leaving no doubt that he was still ravenous for her.

His tongue delved inside to tangle with hers. Shuddering explosions of pleasure jolted her to her core, and her fingers bit into the hardened planes of his shoulders. An overpowering recognition of everything around them—the sea-laced breeze, the silver rays of moonlight that invaded the velvet blackness surrounding them, the balmy feel of the tropical night—heightened her awareness of his virility, the seductive warmth of his nearness.

"You are everything I've always avoided and I've always wanted. Stay the night with me, Mei Li."

CHAPTER SIX

Mei Li pulled back to look searchingly into Michael's eyes. "You're asking for all the wrong reasons." She covered his hands cupping her face with her own. "I can't."

Michael slid his fingers through the silky strands of her hair to clasp the back of her head. He was rushing her, and she was wise enough to realize he was rushing himself as well. He gathered her to him, and they stood on the beach for a long time, letting the waves flow over their bare feet. He would savor this moment of inner contentment forever.

When he finally stepped away, he took her hand in his and said, "You know, you scare the hell out of me, lady. You seem to know me better than I know myself at times."

"I know you're at a crossroad in your life and not sure which way to go."

"And making love will complicate things?"

"Possibly."

He stared down at her for a long moment, then said, "Let's go back and have that dessert now."

They walked back in silence. Leaving Mei Li on the deck, Michael went inside to fix the dessert. When he returned, he was carrying a tray with two halves of a scooped-out pineapple filled with fresh fruit. It was perfect, a light, cool dessert, and Mei Li ate every bite.

After dessert Mei Li announced she had to go or she wasn't sure she would be able to drag herself out of bed the next morning.

"I thought you were a morning person," Michael said laughingly. "People who start the day before sunrise usually are."

"I am a morning person, but every once in a while my five hours of sleep a night catch up with me, and I need more." She wasn't going to tell him that that only occurred when her life was in an emotional upheaval. At the door she stood on tiptoe and kissed him lightly on the mouth. "Thank you for the wonderful dinner. I'll see you at nine."

The moment she left, Michael went into the kitchen and made a pot of coffee. He knew he wasn't going to sleep much that night. With his mug he sat on the deck in the dark and tried to sort through his life. Tonight on the beach just proved to him that he had no business becoming involved with Mei Li. If he had an affair with her, he would only end up hurting her. If he was smart, he wouldn't be there tomorrow morning at nine.

One of Michael's dark eyebrows rose. "I thought you said the beach was off the beaten track. I think I could have found this. Everyone else on Oahu has." He scanned the people at Waimea Bay Beach Park and estimated that at least two hundred people were there, fifty of them associated with Mei Li's family. "And it's not even nine thirty yet. By noon it will be wall-to-wall people."

"Last night while I was at your house, the family gathered and decided to change beaches. They heard about another large family meeting at the other place." Mei Li pulled into the last slot in the parking lot. "I'm afraid today every beach will be crammed."

"I read somewhere that this beach was dangerous." He looked at the water and had to admit it seemed calm enough. Certainly nothing was happening to the swimmers out in the water.

"Only in the winter. The waves can be twenty feet tall here. Then, some of the beaches along this coast are favorite hangouts for surfers." Mei Li loaded Michael down with baskets of food and a large blanket while she carried the net and volleyball.

"You'll have to guide me. Don't let me trip over human bodies," Michael mumbled from behind the mound he was carrying.

He hadn't been on a picnic since he was a child and his parents had been alive. For one fleeting moment he hesitated, sharply remembering that last planned picnic before the raid. He shook the memory from his head and nearly dropped all the food onto the ground at Mei Li's feet. He was not going to ruin this day for her because of his past.

At the picnic site Mei Li quickly ran through the introductions again, and Michael found he could remember who was who in her immediate family but not the thirty relatives and friends who were also there.

"I'd better warn you, my father will continue the interrogation today if you two are left alone," Mei Li said as one of the teenage boys snatched the volleyball net from her hands and raced for the beach.

"I'm curious. What did you tell your parents the other night when I didn't stay for dinner?"

"The truth, of course."

Michael's eyes narrowed. "The truth?"

"That you just remembered a previous obligation. Of course, I didn't mention the previous obligation was with yourself."

"Did they buy it?"

118

"Yes, why wouldn't they? People come and go at my parents' home all the time. It's informal. One more person doesn't throw them."

A frown clouded his eyes. "Yes, well, I was just wondering."

"Why? I thought it didn't matter to you."

He didn't answer right away, and when he did, there was a strange tone to his voice. "I was raised by my Uncle William, and he was very formal. There was a procedure and order to things that had to be followed no matter what. To this day it's hard for me to relate to anything else."

"The only thing that has an order in my life is my gardens."

"To my uncle nothing could be out of place. Needless to say, when he was strapped with a ten-year-old boy, his household was thrown into chaos. But not for long." There was a bitter edge to his words as he thought of that first year of adjustment when he had desperately needed emotional comfort and could find none from William Rutledge.

"You didn't get along with your uncle?" Mei Li wondered what had happened to his parents but sensed the question would be ignored.

"We got along great." The bitterness spilled over into his expression. "As long as I did everything his way, there was no problem. I learned that quite quickly."

"I don't see you conforming."

"Conform? No, not in my mind where it counted. My uncle was a great incentive to get out of there. Thankfully for both of us, I went to college at sixteen before I openly rebelled."

"Sixteen!"

He grinned. "I grew up faster than most kids. For two years before I went to college I attended a military academy, which I hated, but I was able to come home on the weekends, which wasn't much better. When I went away to college, at least I didn't have to answer to my uncle very often."

"You didn't have much of a childhood."

Michael started to say something when he felt a small hand touch his leg. He looked down to find Karin looking up at him.

"Hello." Michael hunched down to the little girl's level.

"Hi, mister. Will you watch me in the water? My mommy and daddy are busy." She pointed to a group of adults trying to anchor everything down so the wind didn't scatter their belongings all over the beach.

Michael's gaze swung to Mei Li's. He wasn't sure what to say.

"My sister won't let her go into the water without an adult accompanying her."

"Please, mister."

He smiled at Karin and said, "Okay." Straightening, he took the little girl's hand in his and whispered to Mei Li, "Help."

Mei Li laughed. "You'll do fine. Karin's a good swimmer for her age."

"That's not what I'm worried about. I don't know the first thing about children."

"You were a child once."

Aeons ago and not for long, Michael thought as he lifted his T-shirt over his head. Thrusting his shirt into Mei Li's hand, he realized she was right about his not having had much of a childhood. As he climbed down the slope to the beach, his gaze sought Mei Li. She was perched on top of the bluff that overlooked the beach. Her long hair caught in the breeze, and its ebony strands danced about her slim, petite figure. Her hands were still clutching his shirt.

Mei Li watched from the crest while Michael and Karin played in the surf. She thought back to the night before when he had asked her to stay with him. She had been tempted, had recklessly wanted to say yes. But she wasn't sure that she could handle a casual affair, and at this moment in his life that was all Michael was willing to have. She wanted all of him. But she wasn't Wonder Woman; it would be hard to refuse the next time.

"Ah, so your young man is back for another dose of the Vandenburgs." Charles came up behind his daughter, peering down at the pair in the water as they rode the gentle waves into shore.

"You aren't going to give him the third degree, are you, Dad?"

"Isn't that what fathers are supposed to do with men their daughters date?"

"I'm not so sure you can say we're dating."

"What are you two doing?"

"Circling."

"I'm suppose to understand that?"

"We're just friends."

"Friends don't look at each other like you two do." He started back toward the rest of the clan. "But I'll keep my questions to a minimum for the time being—until you two realize it's more than friendship between you."

As Michael, with Karin in hand, trudged across the sand and up the slope, Mei Li secured her hair with a rubber band. Oh, she realized it was more than friendship between her and Michael, and she knew he did, too. That was the real problem.

Michael returned Karin to her mother, then walked over to Mei Li. At least he looked

122

none the worse, she thought, watching his eyes flare as they roamed down her length. Not even the wind could cool the heat that flamed her cheeks.

"I don't see any battle scars," she said. Her voice caught when her perusal of him discovered another scar just visible above the waist of his swimming trunks. She clenched her hand to keep from touching the scar and asked, "How did you get that?"

"Nothing heroic or glorious. An operation."

"For your appendix?"

"For a gunshot wound."

"And that one?" Her hand grazed the long scar on his shoulder.

"A confrontation with a knife."

"Oh." Guns and knives were alien to her. She wouldn't even know how to handle them.

He stepped close, his voice low and gruff. "Those are the visible signs of the type of life I led, but there are other scars just as deep and permanent, Mei Li."

"Hey, you two, want to play a game of volleyball? We need two more players," Mei Li's oldest sister shouted at them.

"Yes," Mei Li said quickly, realizing this wasn't the time or the place for this conversation. She handed Michael his shirt and hurried toward the volleyball court on the beach.

Couples were on opposite sides, and Mei Li

found herself facing Michael across the net. As the game started, his intense gaze was riveted to her, but the second the action began he quickly moved, slamming the ball back into Mei Li's court. She dove for the ball, bringing her fisted hands under it to punch it up into the air. Thomas, Karin's father, sent it sailing back over the net.

Again and again Michael and Mei Li were matched against each other, her skill and finesse against his brute force. Once he went up to block a shot and she faked him, hitting it to the side toward her brother-in-law, who spiked it over the net. Another time Mei Li jumped to the side, trying to get under the ball, and lost her balance. She fell into the sand at Michael's feet.

Taking a rare moment to catch her breath, she lifted her head, slowly looking up at him, from his long, muscular legs, over his flat stomach and wide chest, to his face, where his eyes were glinting with humor. He offered her his hand, and she took it. His touch did more to disrupt her normal breathing than the game of volleyball.

With a positively sexy grin on his face, he assisted her to her feet and helped dust off the sand. "I never took you for such a fierce competitor."

"There's a lot you don't know about me yet.

I am a fighter," she warned and dared him at the same time.

Mei Li moved back into position, but she could still feel his hands on her as they brushed the sand off her sweat-drenched body. She lost her concentration and missed the next two plays, both easy shots.

In the end Michael's team won by two points. Mei Li berated herself as she walked off the court and toward the water. Then strong arms captured her and brought her back against a broad, sweat-covered chest.

"What? No kiss for the victor?" Michael whispered into her ear, his breath tickling her neck.

"Don't push your luck, buster, or I'll tell you what I'd like to give you." She had meant to put strength into her words, but they came out teasingly soft and a smile threatened to take hold.

"Ah, something more?"

She arranged her features into a frown—even though it was hard to keep in place—and faced him, stepping back for some breathing room. "You deliberately distracted me. I saw that wink you sent me when I was going for the ball, and then there was that time your hand 'accidently' captured mine under the net. I should have called foul right then and there."

"Why didn't you?" With each step she took backward, he stalked her.

"I don't know. I—" A wave broke over her feet. "It's just a game." Another step back, and the water was up to the calves of her legs. She had a hard time keeping her balance.

"What we're playing isn't a game."

The husky appeal in Michael's voice disarmed her, and she faltered. She lost her footing momentarily and fell back into the water when a wave knocked her off her feet. She came up spluttering, choking on a mouthful of salt water. His large hands steadied her, anchoring her against his strong body.

She felt his manly reaction against her, and her gaze flew to his sardonic face. She felt trapped by his masculine power.

"This is definitely not a game, Mei Li." Still holding her against him, he continued in a menacingly silky voice, "I'm used to taking what I want, when I want. I've never had time to play games. I've never had time for anything but the basics."

"Are you trying to frighten me again?"

"No, educate you. With you, I'm finding that the rules I've gone by don't apply, and I'm not sure I know how to play by your rules."

"There are no rules!"

"Ah—anything goes, then?"

126

"No, that's not what I meant," she declared, frustrated by his infuriating smile, his disconcerting nearness.

"What do you mean? I want you to spell it out for me."

She stiffened her spine and managed to put some space between them. "I mean," she began in a dignified voice, "that in a relationship I don't sit down and think of a list of behavioral rules that we must play by."

"So we're in a relationship," he taunted, his eyes dangerously dark.

"Any two people relating is a relationship."

Michael moved to close the space between them. "And we at least relate on one level." His eyes glinted with his meaning.

"Do we? What I want and what you want are two entirely different things."

"You see? You do have rules."

"No, wants! They're not the same thing."

Mei Li turned and dove into the water. When she surfaced, she started swimming away from shore, away from Michael, who stood in the surf watching her. She wouldn't allow herself to think of anything, especially the devastating effect Michael Rutledge had had on her life in such a short time.

When Mei Li had swam off her frustration and anger, she returned to shore to find Michael involved in another volleyball game.

The earlier victors were playing a challenging team. She sat in the shade of the bluff and watched the game.

There wasn't an ounce of fat on Michael's tall, beautifully proportioned body. His muscles glistened in the noonday sun as he put everything he had into the game. He was the fierce competitor, not her. He fought for every point they won, and she suspected that that was the way he went through life.

When the game was over and Michael's team had won again, he extracted himself from the joyous group and made his way toward her. His impudent and slow tour of her took in her scantily clad body. His eyes told her that he found her seductive.

"I think I'm going to have to throw the next game," he said with a sexy grin. "At this rate I'll be on the beach playing volleyball all afternoon. After lunch we have another challenger."

"You—deliberately lose?" she exclaimed. "This I've got to see."

"I'm not so sure it would be deliberate. My body isn't what it used to be."

She resisted the urge to let her gaze wander down his body. "Oh, I don't see anything wrong with it."

His deep chuckle was husky with passion. "There are a lot of younger men out there who would love to be in the shape you're in. I mean . . ." She blushed, realizing what she was admitting to.

His face radiated with a heart-stopping smile. "Go on. I like what you've said so far."

"Let's eat. I'm starved," she quickly replied, and started to step around him.

He clasped her arm and tugged her to him. His eyes roped hers in an enticing capture. "We can continue this conversation later, when we're alone. We will be alone sometime today, won't we?"

"Yes," she whispered. His sensuous look had robbed her of a strong voice.

He lowered his gaze to the pulse at her throat, breaking the visual chain that had imprisoned her. "It's not every day that I get a beautiful woman to compliment me."

"You're not a man who thrives on compliments."

"There you go again, telling me what kind of man I am. How much experience have you had with men, Mei Li?"

She yanked her arm from his grasp, her eyes darkening with anger. "It's none of your business." She stalked off toward the slope, hating it when he mocked her, furious that he would ask her, because the truth was, she had had very little experience with men. If he knew that, he probably would run scared.

The rest of the afternoon they warily skirted around each other. When they were thrown into the same group, they were polite and civil but cool. Michael played two more volleyball games before his team was defeated. Mei Li noticed he went down fighting to the very end.

By the time they started to pack up and leave, Michael fit right in with her family, joking with her brothers and male cousins, and her female relatives let her know what a catch he was. She felt that jealous streak flare in her, and it took a great deal of effort to remember these people were her family.

"Where to next?"

Michael had come up behind her while she was closing the lid on a basket and whispered the question in her ear. She hadn't even heard him approach. It took a moment for her heart to slow enough so she could answer him. "To the art fair at the resort. And then at sunset there are the fireworks."

"Maybe we can find a quiet spot to watch the fireworks from."

"Quiet spot?" She laughed. "Not where we're going."

Fifteen minutes later he saw what Mei Li was referring to. They were in a long line of cars waiting to go through the gates of the resort.

"Is everyone on the North Shore here?" Michael asked.

"Probably."

Twenty minutes later they finally parked and started walking among the booths at the art fair. They sampled the various foods. Mei Li's favorite was fried bread covered with powdered sugar; Michael's was shaved ice. They were constantly being stopped by someone Mei Li knew. It wasn't until the sun went down that Michael and she had a moment to themselves. They found a semiprivate spot on the beach, spread a blanket, and sat down to wait for the fireworks to begin.

Mei Li drew up her legs, laid her head on her knees, and looked at Michael.

"You said you were raised by your uncle. What happened to your parents?"

"They were killed." The taut set of his features defied her to continue.

"Is your uncle still alive?"

His sharp gaze swerved to her, but he said nothing.

"Is he?" she probed gently.

"Why do you want to know?"

"I think he's part of the reason you're afraid to care too much for someone else," she answered bluntly.

"Yes, he's still alive and quite proud of my accomplishments." Sarcasm was heavy in his

131

voice. "That is, he was up until I quit the State Department last month. It's inconceivable to him that a person would retire from a job at the age of forty."

"But you're not retiring, only changing jobs."

"He doesn't see it that way. My uncle is a government man all the way. He's a retired general, but he still does special assignments from time to time."

He was amazed that he was sitting there talking about his uncle and his childhood with Mei Li. He never talked about them. Once he had walked away from William Rutledge, he was determined that the old man wouldn't shape or influence his life again. By shutting off that part of his life, he had succeeded—at least he had thought he had. But maybe Mei Li was right. Maybe his uncle still had influence over him in a subtle way.

"Have you decided what you're going to do now?"

"Enough, Mei Li."

She straightened, unclasping her legs.

"I don't want to talk about me. I don't want to talk."

The husky timbre in his voice sent her heartbeat speeding. She couldn't see his expression in the growing dark, but what she imagined caused a tingling in the pit of her stomach that rapidly spread through her body.

He gripped her arms and eased her back onto the blanket. Half covering her body with his, he smoothed her hair away from her face.

"I had to share you all day with other people. I will not share you now." He kissed her lightly. "Remember, I was an only child. I never learned to share like you did." Then his mouth captured hers as the fireworks began; a shower of gold illuminated their clasped bodies.

CHAPTER SEVEN

"So the university here would like you to lecture this fall on South American affairs." Lawrence took a sip of his iced tea, watching Michael over the rim of his glass. "Have you accepted the position?"

"No." Michael leaned back against the railing on Lawrence's terrace. The late afternoon sun was slanting through the trees, and the almost constant breeze was warmer than usual.

"It'll be pretty dull compared to what you used to do."

"Maybe that's what I'm looking for."

"Is it? Are you sure you wouldn't be bored out of your mind in one month?"

"No, I'm not sure about much of anything anymore."

"Including Mei Li."

A closed look descended over Michael's features.

Lawrence held up his hand. "Okay. I know I'm butting in when it's none of my business, and I won't say another thing about the job or Mei Li—except that she's the best thing that's happened in my life in years. I needed someone to rejuvenate my will to live my life to the fullest. She wouldn't let me wallow in self-pity."

Michael looked up toward the two-story house and saw someone quickly step back from the window. He couldn't tell who it was because of the glare from the sun. The hairs on the nape of his neck tingled. He swung his gaze back to Lawrence and asked, "Did the mission ever track down your wheelchair?"

"No, but with them it's not that unusual."

"Has anything unusual happened to you since your accident?"

"No. Are you still concerned that someone's trying to kill me?"

Michael shook his head. He had no proof, only a nagging doubt. "Not really." He straightened and placed his drink on the table. "Mei Li should be at my house by now. I'll come by later on this week."

"Ah, to be young again," Lawrence mumbled as Michael walked away.

Michael smiled, a lightness in his stride. Since the pool accident he had visited Lawrence several times. He enjoyed talking to the older man, but no matter what they were discussing the conversation always came around to Mei Li. He strongly suspected Lawrence of matchmaking, even though the older man denied it when Michael had jokingly asked him.

When Michael entered his house, the first thing that always struck him was the fragrance of the fresh flowers that Mei Li made sure were in a bowl on the coffee table every day. The second thing was the profusion of plants—all gifts from Mei Li—in the living room. Every time he stepped through the doorway into his house, he was reminded of the jungle.

In one part of his mind he realized she was taking over his life, and he wasn't sure he liked it. That was his biggest problem: his life was in limbo. He had always had goals in his life until now.

The phone ringing disturbed the quiet of the house. He hurriedly picked up the receiver and said, "Rutledge here."

"Michael, this is Kurt."

Michael frowned but didn't say anything.

"I know you don't want to hear this, but all hell is breaking loose in Costa Sierra. We could use your expertise."

Michael looked about the room at the plants. He thought back over the last several weeks with Mei Li. She brought out a part of himself he hadn't known existed, an easier, more relaxed, gentler side that had been submerged for years. But he still felt like a toddler just learning to walk. He didn't know this new person well enough yet. He wasn't comfortable with himself.

"Michael?"

"Sorry, Kurt, I was thinking."

"I hope about my offer. You can write your own ticket."

"Let me think on it." For some reason he didn't want to refuse outright. He had always been taught to leave as many options open as possible. What if he discovered that the only thing he was really capable of doing was his old job? What if he found his former way of life was all he could manage successfully? Maybe he was too old and set in his ways to change directions now.

"Two weeks is all I can give you. The president of Costa Sierra was admitted to the hospital, and it doesn't look good for him."

"I'll get back to you then." Michael hung up as the doorbell rang.

As Michael answered the door, he realized he would have to think about Kurt's offer later, as well as the university's position.

Mei Li was hidden behind a huge green plant. "Does Mr. Michael Rutledge live here?"

"It depends. Is that for him?"

"Of course. Why else would I break my back holding it?"

Michael laughed. "It takes me half the morning to water the plants you've given me."

"But think of all the oxygen they're giving off in your house," she said as she handed over the new plant to him.

"Do you have any left in your greenhouse?"

"Hundreds."

He started to set the pot down in front of the window that got the afternoon sun.

"No, that plant needs shade."

He found a spot away from the window. "You see, I can't even tell you if these plants need sun or shade. Are you trying to make a gardener out of me? I have to tell you now that I suspect I have a black thumb."

"Nonsense. You just need a little education. A house isn't a home without plants."

"Don't try to change me, Mei Li," Michael warned in a serious voice.

"Change you? All I'm doing is sharing a little of me with you. I love flowers and plants." She glanced about the living room. "I might have gone overboard here, but it wasn't with the intention of changing you. The only person who can do that is you."

His sharp gaze bored into her, and he tried

138

to gauge the real intent behind her words. "Are you ready for your cooking lesson?"

She was becoming used to his changing the subject when it became too uncomfortable, too personal. "I think I should be asking you if you're ready."

"Having second thoughts?" There was a hint of a challenge in his question.

"About learning to cook more than frozen dinners, no. What's on the menu?" she asked as they went into the kitchen.

"A Cantonese seafood noodle dish."

She shot him a surprised look at his choice. "I'll never be able to cook Chinese food as well as my mother."

"Nonsense. You just need a little education —and practice," he threw her own words back at her.

Holding up her hand, she laughed. "Okay, okay. You've made your point." Then impishly she asked, "Are you trying to change me, Michael?"

Ignoring her barb, he took a wok out of the cabinet. "When you cook in a wok, it's fast, and you have to have everything ready beforehand." He went on to explain about the cooking vessel. "The key to this is organization."

"Organization. Got it. Maybe you should

take that job at the university. I think you're a natural born teacher."

He looked at her piercingly. "Are you making fun of me?"

She pointed to herself, a twinkle in her dark eyes. "Who? Me? I know better than that."

His penetrating gaze narrowed even more as he advanced on her. "A student should have proper respect for her teacher."

With laughter dancing in her eyes, Mei Li stepped away from Michael until her back was pressed into the counter. He trapped her with his arms on either side of her, his lower body holding her intimately immobile.

"If you want to eat tonight, you're going to have to prepare it," Michael announced.

"What if I ruin the dinner? That's a definite possibility. You may have a black thumb, but I have a charred thumb. I've been known to burn hot dogs."

"That can happen on the grill, especially if the fire's too hot and you aren't paying close attention."

She smiled sheepishly. "They weren't on the grill. They were in a pan of boiling water. I forgot about them until I smelled something burning. When I finally took then off the stove, all the water had boiled out of the pan."

He tried to suppress his grin, but it broke

140

through his somber expression. "We'll eat whatever you cook."

"You may be eating your words later." Laughter laced her voice until his desirous gaze snared hers. Her throat and mouth went dry, and her heartbeat increased. She ran her tongue over her lips and started to say something.

Michael stilled her words with a finger; then he dipped his head toward her and licked her dry lips. When he drew away, he murmured, "I'll take my chances with you."

Mei Li sensed he meant that on more than one level, and her heart soared with happiness. Over the last few weeks they had spent a lot of time together, and she had seen a gradual easing of his innate alertness. That brooding intensity was still there at times, but he laughed and smiled more.

Entwining her arms around his neck, she pulled him back to her and kissed him, her tongue running over his lips before darting inside his mouth. When she was in his arms, she forgot everything. His kisses stirred her to the tip of her toes, and she couldn't seem to get enough of them.

It was Michael who broke away—something he would never have done in the past. He knew he had to take it slowly with Mei Li, for her as well as himself. But there were occasions like this when he had a hard time remembering his promise to himself concerning Mei Li. Sex could never be taken casually or lightly with her.

"If we don't get started with dinner, it'll be midnight before we eat."

"But don't South Americans eat late? I thought you would be used to a late dinner hour," she teased, realizing that she was getting under his skin. She wanted it to be extremely difficult for him to walk away from her next month when his lease with Kurt was up.

He ignored her and said, "Now, the first thing you need to do is—"

"Wash my hands."

He arched his eyebrow and frowned.

Laughing, she said, "I've been working in the garden."

"Fine. After you wash your hands, you have to combine the oil, salt, and white pepper for the noodles in a bowl and then set it aside. Then you can prepare the sauce."

After Mei Li mixed the sauce and set it aside, Michael handed her the squid to split and score. Aghast, she held the squid up and said, "We're not going to eat this!"

"It's part of the recipe."

"Let's get creative and leave it out."

"Have you ever had squid?"

"No, but—"

"Then we leave it in. You'll be surprised at how good it is in this recipe. Trust me"

"That's a two-way street, Michael," she said, suddenly seriously.

"I know. I'm working on it. But after forty years it doesn't come easy."

She sighed, resigned to the squid and to Michael's slow progress. "Okay, show me how to cut these."

After blanching the broccoli and cooking the noodles to a golden brown, Mei Li fried the seafood. Then the real action started when Michael barked out orders faster than she could keep up.

Halfway through adding the ingredients to the wok, she threw up her hands and said, "Please! Slow down! Five seconds here, ten seconds there. How do you keep it all straight?"

"Stir, Mei Li, or the mushrooms will burn," he commanded.

She saluted and did as he said, mumbling, "I take it back about being a teacher. You should have been a drill sergeant in the Marines."

A few minutes later Mei Li finished by pouring the seafood and vegetable mixture over the Chinese egg noodles on a large platter. She whirled around and presented her dinner to Michael. "Well? How does it look?"

"The question isn't how does it look, but how does it taste."

She produced a spoon. "Then try it."

He tasted the dish, a neutral expression on his face as he laboriously chewed.

"Well?"

"Not bad. The mushrooms are a little overdone, but otherwise it's eatable."

Mei Li couldn't stand it. She had to try her first attempt at a complicated dish. "This is great! You're just jealous that I did so well the first time. Maybe I've missed my calling."

"Don't let one meal go to your head. Julia Child you aren't."

"Yet," she countered saucily, and took the platter out onto the deck where Michael had set the table earlier.

"I think I've created a monster," he said from the doorway.

"Who is ravenous." And without waiting for Michael, she began to spoon the seafood dish onto her plate.

Throughout most of the dinner the conversation was light and casual. But over coffee afterward, Michael said, "Kurt called me tonight right before you came."

"Checking up on his house?"

"No, checking up on its occupant. He wants me to come back and work at my old job."

"And?"

"I told him I would think about it."

"Why are you having second thoughts about quitting now?"

"Because I'm not sure who I am. At least in my old job I knew."

"I could tell you what kind of man you are, but it's something you must find out for yourself. The unknown is always scary. Some people never change because of that."

Capturing her hand on the table, Michael rubbed his thumb across her palm. "What's scary is your perception. I'm not sure I want someone to know me better than I know myself."

When he took her chin between his thumb and forefinger, he pulled her toward him to brush his lips across hers. Running his fingers through her silky hair, he deepened the kiss.

As Michael trailed tiny kisses to her earlobe, Mei Li said breathlessly, "I hear the phone."

"Let it ring," he muttered as he nipped lovingly on the shell of her ear.

"Please! I can't stand to let a phone ring."

Michael grumbled the whole way into the house and practically growled into the phone when he picked it up.

"Yes, she's here." He held the receiver out for Mei Li. "It's Charlie."

Her brother wouldn't have called unless something was wrong. Her hand trembled as she took the phone from Michael. "What's happened?"

"Dad. He's drunk and insists on seeing you."

The urgency in her brother's voice alarmed Mei Li. "Where?" She had never seen her father drink anything stronger than tea.

"At the boat."

"Why, Charlie?"

"They're repossessing the boat tomorrow."

"I'll be right there."

She quietly replaced the receiver in its cradle, her hand still shaking. The boat was her father's life.

"Mei Li? What's wrong?" Michael placed his hands on her shoulders and turned her around to face him. He lifted her chin and looked tenderly into her eyes. "Can I help?"

"Dad lost the boat today. He's drunk and wants to see me."

"I'll go with you. You might need some help."

"You don't have to. Charlie is there."

"I want to, if you'll let me."

"Thanks. I'm not sure how to deal with this."

As they left the house, Mei Li explained that her father was at the boat dock, not at home. At Halelwa she directed Michael to the pier where her father kept his charter boat, realizing that her father had come this way every morning all these years. Even if he didn't have a charter, he was always down at the pier, working on the boat or talking with other charter boat captains.

Charlie greeted them. "He's down below. I've gotten him to stop drinking, but he keeps ranting and raving that this is all Lawrence Harris's fault."

Puzzled, Mei Li said, "Lawrence doesn't have anything to do with the finance company."

"I tried to tell Dad that. He won't listen. Says he has to talk to you."

Mei Li boarded the boat and went down the stairs into the cabin. Her father lay sprawled on a bunk, his eyes closed. Suddenly his eyelids flew open, and he turned his reddened gaze on her.

"You have to get out of there."

Mei Li moved to the bunk. "Out of where?"

"Lawrence's."

"Why, Dad?"

He gripped her hand and pulled himself up to a sitting position. "He's bad news. Has been ever since I met him. Look what he's done to

147

Hawaii. Such a beautiful, unspoiled place when I first came." His words were slurred but forceful.

"Dad, Lawrence hasn't spoiled Hawaii. His land projects have always preserved the area around them."

"Too many people here. Too many tourists."

"Those tourists are the same people who charter your boat."

His eyelids slid closed as he lay back down. "Lost her," he mumbled, defeat in his voice.

"Go to sleep. I'll be here."

"Lawrence tried to ruin my life," Charles mumbled, but his voice faded as he drifted off into sleep.

Mei Li waited until she was sure her father was asleep before going up on deck. "Charlie, I'll stay with him. Go on home."

"Dad kept rambling about Mr. Harris ruining his life—something about taking his career away. I don't want you to work for that man," her brother announced vehemently, a scowl on his face.

"Charlie, I'm not making any decisions until I know all the facts. I'll talk with Dad when he's sober."

Her brother climbed up onto the pier. "You just do that. All I know at the moment is that Lawrence Harris is responsible for turning this family upside down and inside out." He pointed his finger toward the passageway to the cabin, saying, "This isn't like Dad at all, and I'm really worried." Then he stormed away.

Mei Li drew in a sharp breath. "Charlie is right about one thing. I do feel like this family is falling apart." She turned toward Michael, tears shimmering in her almond-shaped eyes. "I don't want to quit my job at Lawrence's. Am I being selfish?"

Michael gathered her into the shelter of his arms. "I think you should wait until you know all the facts. I've never been one to make rash decisions about important matters."

"It may be all night before Dad wakes up. Are you sure you want to stay?"

"Yes." His arms tightened about her. "I want to be here for you if you need my help." It wasn't often he had the luxury of being able to help out a friend. Usually he was so involved in his work, he was never around.

The tropical air, the ocean breeze, and the semidarkness lent an intimacy to the situation that was hard to ignore. Mei Li wanted to forget why she was there and concentrate on the passion that Michael stirred in her. But her father's presence was always in the back of her mind. She had never been able to walk away from problems. They had to be dealt with and solved. She had to come up with a solution that would satisfy her father and herself as well.

"Let's sit," Michael gently commanded, already guiding her over to a set of cushioned chairs used for fishing. "Tell me about growing up in a large family."

"A constant battle for what was yours. No privacy. Sharing a room, clothes, toys. But you always knew someone was there for you when you needed them. There was—still is—a lot of love in my parents' house. How about you? Before you went to live with your uncle."

From the light that spilled from below deck, Mei Li could see Michael's tension and the nerve that twitched in his cheek when he was upset.

"My parents were missionaries. We traveled a lot into back countries," he replied curtly.

"How were they killed? An accident?"

"No."

The finality in his voice demanded an end to the conversation. Silence reigned between them, until Mei Li looked up to find her father standing in the doorway to the cabin, clutching at the hatch to support most of his weight. She bolted to her feet and rushed over to him.

"Dad, you should be lying down."

He pushed away from her and staggered

toward a chair, plopping down into it with his legs sprawled out in front of him. "Don't tell me what to do, girl. You won't listen to me, so why should I listen to you?"

Mei Li sat down in the chair next to her father's. "Please, Dad."

"Do you know the last time I had a drink of liquor?"

"No." Mei Li was aware of Michael moving behind her and welcomed his reassuring hand on her shoulder.

"In 1947. Never touched another drop until tonight. He's destroyed my life again."

Mei Li frowned. "He?"

"Lawrence Harris." Her father spat the name out, distaste stamped into his weathered features.

"Lawrence doesn't have anything to do with the finance company. He's in real estate."

Her father turned a furious gaze on her. "The hell he doesn't! Who do you think owns the finance company? Harris Enterprises is the holding company. I found that out today."

Mei Li hid her surprise, trying to remain calm for her father's sake. "Then I'll speak with Lawrence. I'm sure something can be worked out."

Her father's hand came down hard on the

arm of the chair. "No, you won't! I will not take a handout from that bastard."

Mei Li knelt in front of her father and grasped his hands. "Please tell me why, Dad. He's been good to me."

Her father flinched as if he had been hit. "It's his guilty conscience and the fact that you're your mother's daughter."

More puzzled than ever, Mei Li asked, "What does Mother have to do with this?"

"He was in love with her. We both were, back in 'forty-seven, while we were stationed at Pearl Harbor. Harris was my commanding officer, and I was just a lowly seaman." His voice faded, and he closed his eyes wearily.

Mei Li swallowed the tight ache in her throat and asked in a quavering voice, "What happened?"

Her father's eyes opened, and he seemed to stare right through her to another time, another place. "I got drunk one night and beat him up. I couldn't take any more of him coming around and courting your mother, talking against me, filling her head with lies. Yeah, I drank too much on occasion, but so did a lot of other guys."

"You beat up your commanding officer?"

"I didn't know what I was doing. I tried to apologize later, but he had me brought up on charges. I had to serve some time, and I've had to live with that on my record ever since. I'm not a criminal. I didn't deserve a dishonorable discharge." A bitter laugh filled the air. "But I did end up with your mother. That's the only time I've bested that man."

Mei Li slowly rose, stunned by the news. Shaking her head, she tried to gather her poise about her, but she couldn't. Shuddering, she went into Michael's embrace.

"Such hatred and bitterness," she whispered.

Michael ran his hand soothingly up and down her back. "Revenge and honor can be strong emotions."

Mei Li pulled back and looked up at Michael. He spoke from experience, and she wanted to ask him about it, but her father stumbled to his feet. He swayed. Michael started forward, but her father caught himself before falling.

As he plodded toward the cabin, he muttered, "I'll get even with Lawrence Harris if it's the last thing I do."

Alarmed at the venom in her father's voice, Mei Li began to follow her father. Michael caught her wrist and tugged her back against him, anchoring her against him.

"No, let him sleep it off. Tomorrow he probably won't even remember what he said tonight."

Glancing toward the passageway, Mei Li murmured, "But the feelings toward Lawrence will still be there."

She sensed that her father knew exactly what he had said.

CHAPTER EIGHT

The next day Mei Li still felt numb from her father's revelations concerning Lawrence. Nothing that Chang had taught her through the years quite prepared her to handle this situation. One part of her felt betrayed, but she wasn't even sure by whom. Another part of her felt pity that revenge and anger could affect people's lives so strongly and for so long.

"Mei Li, I didn't expect you today. What a pleasure." Lawrence wheeled himself closer to where she sat on a stone bench in the garden.

She had always been honest and direct with Lawrence in the past; she wouldn't stop now. "I'm not sure you'll feel that way after you know why I came by."

Lawrence looked long and hard at Mei Li. "You know," he whispered, sadness taking away the bright gleam in his eyes.

"Dad told me last night."

"I knew it would only be a matter of time before you found out what happened between your father and me."

"Were you in love with my mother?"

He nodded.

Never once in all the time they had talked had he mentioned her mother other than in a polite, distant way. "Did you give me the job because of my mother?"

The sadness in his eyes deepened. "No, I almost didn't give you the job because of Jade. I didn't know if I could handle seeing you every day. You look so much like your mother. She was a beautiful, gentle woman." His voice softened; he stared into space, reliving another time. "She still is."

"Then you were responsible for my father's dishonorable discharge from the navy," Mei Li murmured.

"No, he was."

"But you brought charges against him!"

"He put me in the hospital," Lawrence countered, a hard edge to his voice.

"Was it that or the fact that my mother loved him?"

"To be honest, probably both. But the overriding factor was that as an officer I had to retain command of my men. I could never

156

allow them to feel they could attack an officer and get away with it."

"So you tried to ruin my father's life. The sea was his home!"

Scowling, Lawrence leaned forward. *"He* ruined his chances in the navy. *He* was the one who got drunk and attacked me."

Mei Li rose with as much dignity as she could muster. *"He* is my father."

"Mei Li, it was a long time ago." Lawrence sagged back in his wheelchair with a heavy sigh. "I'm willing to forget the past. Your father is the one who won't let go of it."

"Is that why Harris Enterprises is repossessing his boat?" Her hands curled into a tight ball at her sides.

"What?" Lawrence jerked upright.

"You took my father's boat away," she accused angrily.

She whirled around and started to leave. But she stopped when she saw Michael a few feet away. She desperately fought the tears that choked her.

"I'll be in the car," she said finally to Michael and hurried past him.

At his car she leaned onto it and drew in deep breaths to still her racing heart. A month ago her life had been orderly and peaceful. Now she wasn't sure of anything.

"Mei Li, are you all right?"

She nodded, her throat still tight.

"Do you want to go to the beach?"

She nodded once again and climbed into Michael's car.

They didn't say a word until Michael parked the car at the state recreational area. He twisted toward her, sliding his arm along the back seat and gathering her to him.

"Do you want to talk about what happened this morning with Lawrence?" Michael asked gently against the top of her hair while he ran his hand up and down her back in soothing caresses.

"I can't. I don't know what I feel. I've never been this angry at someone."

"Lawrence? Or your father?"

"Lawrence should have told me. Why is he taking my father's boat? I could have worked something out with him. I could have worked for him for free." She pulled away from Michael. "Something! Anything! But not what he did to my father."

He laid his hand against her cheek and felt the heat of her anger beneath his palm. "There are always two sides to a situation. Have you listened to Lawrence's?"

"No." She stared down at her clasped hands. "I didn't give him much of a chance to say anything."

"I know you might not like hearing this, but

your father isn't guiltless. He did some things wrong, too."

"But for Lawrence to take my father's boat! Don't you think he's paid enough for that mistake? I don't know what my father will do without his boat. That and his family are his whole life."

"It seems to me Lawrence was surprised by that information. Talk to him. See what he has to say about the loan and the incident with your father."

When she thought over the scene in the garden, she realized Michael was right. Lawrence had been confused, as if he hadn't known what she was talking about when she told him about her father's boat.

"I will when I've calmed down." She smiled faintly, turning slightly to kiss the palm of his hand.

He chuckled. "I thought I was the only one who brought out your anger."

"That isn't the only thing you bring out in me." She couldn't explain the chemistry between them. It had existed from the very beginning.

"If I ignore that comment, we might make it to the beach today."

"And if you don't?" she teased, her hand splayed across his chest. She felt the quickening of his heartbeat.

"We might shock a few people."

Mei Li scanned the parking lot. "There aren't many cars here. Looks pretty deserted to me."

"Is that an invitation?"

"Yes. Kiss me." She curled her fingers into his thick hair and pulled his head down toward hers.

She had always been such an even person until she had met Michael. The intensity of her emotions lately still surprised her. He provoked anger, passion, and boldness in her. She was falling in love with him and wasn't sure if it was a wise thing to do.

He pressed her to his solid chest, their heartbeats racing as one. As she tilted her head back, his lips erotically explored the long column of her neck, and she clung to him for support.

It would be so easy to give in to her emotions and forget where they were. Michael had the power to wipe away all rational thoughts and leave her mind centered on the sensual sensations he produced in her.

When he lifted his head, his gaze caught and held hers. Their raggedly expelled breaths merged in the small space that separated them as they continued to stare at each other. Then they came together again; the hot interplay of their mouths made them oblivious to their surroundings as they sought to please and be pleased.

"Get out of the car," demanded a rough voice from outside the car.

Michael jerked away from Mei Li. Through the window on the passenger's side a burly man pointed a gun at Mei Li's head. Michael silently cursed himself for not being more alert.

"I said get out. Now!" The man yanked the door open.

"Michael?"

"Do as he says," Michael said tersely.

"No funny moves, or she gets it." The large man directed the words at Michael.

Mei Li slid out of the car, followed by Michael. Standing, she backed up against Michael, her body shaking with fear, her eyes glued to the gun. Chills swept through her despite the hot summer sun.

"Move!" The man gestured with the gun.

Michael and Mei Li trudged up the sandy incline toward the beach. In the shade of the ironwoods stood another couple with a short man, not more than five feet four inches tall, holding them at gunpoint.

"Over there." The burly man indicated that Michael and Mei Li were to stand next to the other couple.

"What do you want?" Michael asked.

"Shut up," the short man shouted. His eyes were glassy, as if he were on drugs.

Mei Li was amazed that Michael's voice was calm and even, with not a trace of fear in it. He might be used to a gun being pointed at him, but she certainly wasn't. She shuddered again and again as she watched the large man calmly speak in low tones to the shorter one.

Michael didn't like the fact that the short man was extremely nervous. That made for a more precarious situation since he was likely to shoot and ask questions later. Michael had to do something soon, but he knew that once he made his move he wouldn't have a second chance.

He was angry as hell at himself for not being more alert to his surroundings. A few weeks before, this would never have happened. He would never have lost concentration so totally that he wouldn't be aware of a gunman's approach. Now because of his lack of awareness Mei Li was in grave danger. If anything happened to her, he would never forgive himself.

"Please let us go," the other woman whined.

"I said shut up!" the short man exclaimed, sweat beading his forehead. He started for the woman with his arms raised, as if he were going to hit her.

The burly man quietly said, "Billy."

"Why not? What's he going to do?" Billy pointed his gun at the man with the woman.

"Business before pleasure," the burly man reminded his companion.

"Oh, yeah. Money. We want all your valuables." He waved his gun in the air, but when he stopped, it was aimed at Mei Li's heart. "Starting with you. Empty your bag."

"I don't have any money," Mei Li said in a quavering voice.

"Open your bag!" The short man's voice reverberated through the ironwoods.

Mei Li's hands shook as she tried to untie the cord of her bag. She yanked on the strings and only managed to tighten them more. Impatiently the short man moved closer to her. Her head was bent over the bag as she desperately tried to do what he ordered, but she saw his feet in front of her shifting nervously back and forth. She couldn't loosen the strings; she lifted her frightened gaze to Michael's.

The short gunman took another step closer. "You don't follow directions very well. Maybe I should teach you what happens to people who don't."

The burly man hurried over to calm his buddy. Taut with alertness, Michael watched them, calculating the best time to make his move. The little bastard wouldn't lay a finger on Mei Li, or all his years of training were for nothing.

When Michael moved, it was so fast that Mei Li gasped in surprise. Michael struck the short man behind his neck and at the same time he kicked out at the burly man, catching him in the jaw. The short man collapsed to the sand at Mei Li's feet while the large one staggered back, grasping his jaw with one hand, momentarily stunned by the blow. But he remained standing.

Instantly Michael lunged for the man, not giving him a chance to raise his gun. Their bodies, clasped in a warriors' embrace, slammed to the ground. They rolled over as they wrestled for the gun. The man was bigger, but Michael was in better condition. He managed to pin the assailant to the sand and tried to make him release the gun.

"Get that gun, Mei Li!" Michael commanded in a voice that she had never heard before.

For a few seconds Mei Li remained frozen, watching the struggle before her. By the time Michael's words registered on her shocked mind, the other man had grabbed the short robber's gun and was pointing at Michael and the burly man.

"I've got it!" he told Michael.

The burly robber, acknowledging his defeat, let go of his gun. But while everyone was looking at the large man and Michael on the ground, no one noticed the shorter one regain consciousness. He rose behind Mei Li, flipped out his butterfly knife, and quickly took hold of her with his arm across her chest while the knife was pointed at the group.

"I'll kill her if you make one more move toward me," the short man said.

Having risen, Michael whipped around to face Mei Li and the terror on her face. In that moment he knew he could kill again. Everything about him became implacably ruthless as the old Michael resurfaced, the Michael who had faced and survived similar situations before.

Mei Li stared at the knife blade that glinted in the sunlight filtering through the ironwoods. She had read about muggings like this, but nothing had prepared her for dealing with it when she was involved. Her assailant tightened his hold, crushing her into his chest and threatening to cut off her next breath. She tried to draw air into her lungs, but they burned with each shallow breath.

Holding the gun on the short man, Michael said in a menacing voice, "You're a dead man if you harm her. If I have to, I'll hunt you down and kill you with my bare hands."

Mei Li's eyes widened. Michael's expression was blank, but his tone of voice conveyed his deadly intention.

"Drop those guns. Now!" the burly man shouted in a near panic, sweat streaming down his round face. "I'll kill her if you don't. I have nothing to lose."

The other man tossed his gun away. But Michael still held his; his eyes were narrow and piercing as he gauged the man who had Mei Li.

"I said drop the gun!" The burly man waved the knife in a wide arc in front of Mei Li.

Michael began to do as the robber ordered, but instead of throwing the gun away, he raised it, aimed, and shot the man in the arm that held the knife.

The man instantly dropped the knife, howling with pain as he clasped his wound. Mei Li nearly fell from her sudden release but caught herself.

With his gun trained on both assailants, Michael grabbed the knife from the sand. "You're damned lucky I didn't blow your head off."

Numb, Mei Li turned her head to look at the robbers and Michael. She saw the man's blood on her arm and her legs buckled, but Michael caught her before she collapsed.

Anchoring her against him, he held the gun on the two men.

"If you're smart, which I seriously doubt, you won't move a muscle," Michael said in a chilling voice.

"I need a doctor," the injured man whined. "You could have killed me."

"You're right there." He turned to the other victims. "I'll keep these two occupied while you and your wife find a phone and call the police," he said.

After the couple had left, Michael asked, "Are you all right, Mei Li?"

"Yes," she answered in a faint voice.

"Sit down by that tree while I watch these two."

She wasn't sure she could make it to the tree by herself. Her legs felt like jelly, her head was spinning, and her heart was beating frantically.

"I'll stay here." She clung to Michael for support.

He spared her a quick glance and didn't like what he saw. Her face was ashen, and her eyes were large, her pupils dilated.

"Come on. You need to sit down," Michael commanded in a gentle voice as he led her over to the tree while keeping his attention on their two assailants. "Lean back against the trunk. Close your eyes and take deep breaths.

I have everything under control. Those men aren't going anywhere."

Mei Li did as Michael said. Listening to his soothing voice calmed her a bit, but she wouldn't look at the blood on her sleeve.

Her uncle had often told her to think of beautiful things when she was upset. She tried the technique now. Thinking about the gardens she worked in, she managed to hold the terror at bay.

When the police arrived, Mei Li was calmer and was able to give her account of what happened to an officer. but Michael saw the strain on her face and heard the expressionless voice she used. He was worried.

By the time everything was cleared up and they were able to leave, it was nearly seven o'clock. Michael was glad he was finally able to take Mei Li home. She hadn't said a word besides answering the policemen's questions.

After stowing their things in the back of his car, Michael opened Mei Li's door, saying, "Let's have our picnic somewhere else."

"Fine," she replied, her voice flat, her expression neutral.

His worry heightened. He needed to get her home to familiar, safe surroundings.

When Michael started the car, Mei Li said vehemently, "I need to change. I need to take a bath. I need . . ." Then the trembling began, first in her hands, but it spread quickly throughout her body.

Michael switched off the engine and drew her to him, holding her as tightly as possible. He tried to absorb her shudders into his body.

When she pulled back, her eyes shimmering with unshed tears, she rubbed at her arm where the blood had caked on her shirt. "I feel so dirty." Then suddenly she yanked her shirt up over her head and flung it out the window. Underneath she had on her bathing suit top. "I should have done that hours ago."

Michael could see the fire return to her eyes, the color to her cheeks. "It's a normal reaction to something violent."

"But not for you. You're so calm and in control. How can you be?"

His smile was self-mocking. "I've been there many times, Mei Li. You haven't."

"Never." She shook her head as if to deny what had happened.

"We'll eat all this food at your apartment. Confidentially, I have an ulterior motive for going to your place. Do you realize I've never been there?" He interjected a light tone into his voice, trying to get back the easygoing, relaxed person he had been for the last few weeks. But out there on the beach he had effortlessly stepped back into his old role. All his instincts and timing had been keen; he had been ready to kill if necessary.

On the way to Mei Li's he kept up a running dialogue on anything he could think of that was amusing. He told her of some of the pompous people he met in Washington, D.C., who thought the world was made for them. He told her of the hostesses vying to outdo each other with lavish parties.

At her apartment building Mei Li said, "I thought you were never in Washington long."

"I wasn't, but when I was there, I was asked to every party that was worth going to. I think Kurt put an ad in the paper informing Washington when I would be in town. I was unattached, which made me an attractive addition to a party. Then too, you wouldn't believe the information you can pick up at those parties. I'm sure that was why Kurt was so concerned that I wasn't lonely."

"Oh, just doing your duty."

"Yeah," he said with a mischievous grin.

"I bet Kurt had to twist your arm."

"I've got the bruises to prove it."

"Are you going back?"

His grin faded. "I don't know."

"I got an idea how good you were today, Michael. Most people couldn't have acted as quickly as you. No wonder Kurt wants you back."

He placed his hand on the door handle. "If we don't eat our food soon, it'll be ruined." He opened his door and began emptying the back of the car.

Inside Michael was inundated by all the plants that Mei Li had. He felt accosted by the color green. "When do you find time to water all these? I have my hands full with the few you gave me," he said when she came out of her bedroom, having changed out of her bathing suit and into a pair of shorts and a brightly colored shirt.

"When you care, there's time. Let's spread the blanket out on the living-room floor and eat here."

"Why not? It'll seem like we're outside." He opened the blanket and spread it over the floor.

"What else would you expect from a gardener?" Mei Li asked as she took the food out of the picnic basket. She realized that it was just as important for Michael to forget about those two men as for her.

"I've learned not to expect anything from people. That way you aren't disappointed."

"A hard case of cynicism. I suppose I expect too much from people."

"A hard case of romanticism."

"Guilty as charged." She picked up a drumstick and started eating.

171

"Two opposing views."

"It's not surprising. We've lived two very different lives."

She didn't have to tell him that. The incident at the beach had boldly underlined that fact. He had seen her reaction to his voice when he threatened that gunman. He had seen her shock when he shot the man, inches from her.

"You know, I'm curious about one thing." Mei Li finished her chicken and took another piece.

"Only one thing?"

"The other things, you have made clear, are off limits."

"What is it?"

"How did you know that couple was married? She didn't have on a wedding ring."

"You noticed?" He arched a brow in surprise.

"Not till later, when the police were there."

"He had on a wedding band. I took an educated guess that he wouldn't wear his unless the woman he was with was his wife."

"You're not eating," Mei Li said, holding up the container with the fried chicken in it.

He tried to smile but failed. "I see you are. Everything okay now?"

"Yes. You're here. It's behind me. Thinking

about it does no good," she said, trying to sound brave.

"The past is the past?"

"Yes. You can't relive it. Only the present is worth worrying about."

Michael took a piece of chicken from the container and began to eat. But he wasn't hungry. He had too many things to think over. He was so damned confused. Most of the time he didn't know which way he was going. He thought he had started to figure things out —until that afternoon at the beach. It had reinforced what he had been trained to do most of his life.

Finally, when he knew it was useless to try to eat, he rose from the blanket. "I'd better be going, Mei Li."

She stood, placing a restraining hand on his arm. "Please don't go. Stay the night."

CHAPTER NINE

Michael turned around and stared down at Mei Li. Her fingers against his skin felt like an electric bolt. She appeared fragile, easily broken in that moment to him, and his heart twisted. He wanted to reach out to her, hold her tightly to him, and never let her go. But he knew he wouldn't.

"I don't want to be alone after . . . I don't . . ." Her voice trailed off into silence. Tears glistened in her almond-shaped eyes, but she wouldn't cry in front of him. She swallowed hard and dropped her hand back to her side, wishing she had the right to go into his arms and make emotional demands on him.

She started to turn away when Michael captured her arm and pulled her back around to face him. He laid his hand against her cheek; his thumb moved in caressing circles over her skin.

He wanted to wipe the fear and distress

completely from her eyes. He wanted to make love to her badly, but he wouldn't do anything about it. It wasn't because he was a particularly noble person. He just wasn't ready for the kind of deep commitment that Mei Li needed. And she had been through an emotional upheaval on the beach. He would not take advantage of her vulnerability just to satisfy his desire.

"I don't think it would be a good idea," Michael said in a husky voice, filled with the passion that he was so desperately trying to deny existed between them.

"Please. I can make a bed up in here on the couch. Charlie says it's quite comfortable to sleep on." She attempted a shaky laugh. "He should know. He's fallen asleep on it enough in the past." She searched his closed expression and added, "But I'll understand if you want to go." She needed him, but he had to need her, too.

Watching her try to be so brave and fearless made his chest constrict as if he couldn't get a decent breath. If he stayed, he didn't know if he could keep his hands off her; it was always hard to when he was around her. But a few nights of passion weren't for a woman like Mei Li. She deserved a lifetime of love.

"You're safe here, Mei Li."

"I know that in my head. But not in my

heart. Those men made me feel so vulnerable to the evil in the world. You know the saying —'it can't happen to me.' Well, it did happen to me."

Michael could no longer resist his impulse to draw her to him and hold her tightly. His arms sheltered her against the outside world. "If only I could have protected you from that. I should have been able to."

Mei Li heard the self-reproach in his voice and looked up into his face, wanting to erase the creases on his brow and the harsh set of his jawline but knowing she couldn't. "You couldn't do anything to prevent that. You can't blame yourself."

"I should have heard that man approaching the car."

"If I remember correctly, we were preoccupied. You can't spend your whole life on the alert for danger that usually never happens."

"The hell I can't. I was trained for that."

"Michael, what happened on that beach was an exception to the rule, not the rule."

"Not in my world."

"But in mine," she whispered.

They stared at each other for a long time, and the differences between them seemed as wide as an ocean and as difficult to bridge. It didn't alter the fact that Mei Li was in love with him, but it certainly complicated the situation. He would latch on to it and see it as an insurmountable barrier; she saw it as a challenge to be faced.

"Will you stay?" Mei Li broke the silence.

He nodded, knowing he couldn't refuse her that. He would give her the secure feeling she needed to make it through the night, but tomorrow he had some thinking to do—alone, away from her enticing presence.

Michael helped Mei Li clean up the food. Not a word was spoken between them that wasn't necessary. He had completely withdrawn from her, and Mei Li didn't know how to reach him. His unreadable expression was firmly in place, as it had been so many times in the past.

Exhausted from the previous night on the boat and the day's events, Mei Li decided to go to bed early. But she intended to talk about the beach incident with Michael the next day. It had activated some feelings in him that he was wrestling with. She wanted to help him deal with those feelings. If he couldn't trust her with his emotions, then she realized they really hadn't progressed beyond that first day they had met on the beach at Lawrence's.

After making up the couch for Michael, Mei Li paused in her bedroom doorway and said, "Good night."

Sitting down on the couch, he mumbled his

good night and watched her leave the room. When she closed her bedroom door, he glanced about him. He felt as if he had returned to the jungle, surrounded by all her green plants and flowers. The feeling was suddenly disconcerting.

He surged to his feet and flipped on the television, but there was nothing on of interest. Turning it off, he began to pace from one end of the room to the other, feeling as if he were in a cage. He fought the strong urge to leave, because Mei Li needed him. But he didn't think he could sleep, despite his exhaustion.

After prowling the room until he knew every inch of it, he sat back down on the couch and glanced through a book on gardening, not really seeing any of the words or pictures before him. It was just something to do with his hands. When he was finished scanning the book, he lay back on the couch and stared at the ceiling, trying to bring some kind of order to his chaotic thoughts.

But all he could do was relive that scene on the beach. He went over and over what he should have done to prevent those men from taking him and Mei Li in the first place. He should have been able to do something.

Finally sleep took over, and Michael was whisked into the world of dreams. . . .

The day promised to be hot and humid, but he didn't mind. His parents and he were going on a picnic down by the river where they could watch the African animals come to drink.

He had sneaked off from the village to collect some berries to surprise his mother. He was the luckiest boy alive. Every day was an adventure in the jungle. He loved the animals; he loved to explore the strange world with Keeshan, their manservant.

As he headed back to the compound, shouts, then an unearthly scream alerted him that something wasn't right. He dropped his bucket and started to run toward the village. But when he saw smoke billowing into sky, he slowed and cautiously approached the jungle compound. Some innate sense warned him of danger.

He hid in the thick cover of underbrush and looked into the compound. What he saw paralyzed him with fear. Soldiers, revolutionists, had swept through his village, killing and plundering, setting fire to the huts. Their laughter rang hideously in the clearing. He clamped his hands over his ears and shook his head violently, wanting desperately to refute what he was hearing and seeing.

He needed to move, to do something to stop them, but his body was frozen with terror. And as quickly as the soldiers had come, they moved out of the village, having tired of their sport of killing defenseless people.

If you ever want to overcome fear you must face it, son.

Slowly, almost hypnotically, he crawled from the thick underbrush that had sheltered him and walked toward his parents' burning hut. Flames shot upward through the thatched roof; smoke poured through the open windows. Tears stung his eyes and clogged his throat.

"Mom. Dad," he whispered.

He blinked, breaking the mesmerizing spell he was locked in. His stunned attention was riveted to what used to be the front door of his home.

"Mom! Dad!" he shouted frantically above the noise of the crackling fire. His steps quickened; his feet pounded the packed dirt.

Racing toward the burning hut, he fell. The hard ground knocked the breath from him. He tried to take deep breaths to calm his thundering heartbeat, but the smoke-saturated air seared his lungs. Bolting to his feet, he began to move quickly forward again, his cry rising above the sounds of the raging flames.

Mom! Dad! I'll save you.

A white-hot wall of heat blocked him from

his objective. Shielding his face with his raised arms, he tried to look inside, but a barrier of flames and smoke obstructed his view. Tears cascaded down his cheeks as he backed away, his eyes round with shock.

A man doesn't cry, Dad. Keeshan told me.

He wiped his hand across his tear-streaked cheeks.

When you're hurting, son, it's all right to cry.

In that hellish second he knew his parents were dead, and something snapped inside him. Clutching his arms to his chest, he doubled over. Waves of pain ripped through him, driving the shock away and replacing it with harsh reality.

I should have done something! I should have been here to help fight!

He whirled around, wanting to strike out at someone, anyone. His small hands fisted as his dark gaze darted about the village. He was totally alone; he knew in his gut that no one else was alive.

As his gaze flew from one still body to the next, from one burning hut to the next, his tears died inside him, buried deep in his heart.

Why are they killing, Dad?

Some men only know how to kill to get what they want.

181

And the men who had stormed into the village had wanted his missionary parents silenced. A stone wall, thick and high, encircled his heart, his emotions. The word for them was terrorist—not patriots, as they claimed.

He spun toward a crashing sound, crouching low, ready to spring forward—ready to fight, to hurt as he had been hurt. The roof of his parents' hut collapsed into the blaze. As he stared at the flames, something began to change inside of him.

Standing alone in the middle of the village, surrounded by senseless destruction, he made a slow circle, his eyes narrow, his jaw clenched. "They will pay for this," he vowed, straightening, as if trying to appear older than his ten years.

Then suddenly he was struck anew with fear. What if the men came back? What if someone stayed behind and was watching him now? Panicked, he again scanned the jungle compound, his heart pounding against his chest, sweat drenching him. But its very emptiness this time was a comforting balm.

His survey of the ravished village came to a halt at the garden. Food. He looked toward the jungle, where he knew he had to hide, then back toward the garden at the edge of the dense undergrowth. If he were careful, he could use the food from the garden until someone came for him.

Slowly, one by one, his survival instincts were born and sharpened as he moved through the village doing what he must.

But when he found his mother's body behind their hut, everything came rushing in on him. He stood staring at her, unable to move. The stifling, humid air pressed down upon him, and he sucked in deep breaths, but he couldn't seem to get enough.

He had to bury his mother; it was his responsibility. Tearing his gaze away from her, he glanced up. It was growing late. Soon it would be dark. There was no time left for him to be afraid, to feel the pain, to grieve.

He looked back down at his mother on the ground and took one step closer. Then another. He reached down to turn her over. . . .

Quaking, Michael sat up, blinking, trying to determine where he was. All he saw in the dark shadows of night was plants. Disoriented, he sprang off the couch, knocking something over onto the floor.

A light came on. Blinking, Michael stared at the doorway where Mei Li was. Their gazes locked. She was a vision of softness, something he had had little of in his life. He resisted her appeal and looked away.

"Michael, what's wrong?" She was beside him instantly, touching his T-shirt. "You're soaking wet."

He raked his hand through his damp hair, over and over. But all he could think was: *I should have done something.*

"Please, Michael. Tell me what happened. You're shaking." Her voice was full of concern and alarm. She placed her hand on his arm, but he pulled away, putting several feet between them.

Michael looked down and found the garden book lying on the floor. Bending over, he picked it up. It gave him something to do. It gave him time to compose himself so he could answer Mei Li.

When he finally spoke, his voice was even, calm. "Just a bad dream. Nothing important." He shrugged, appearing completely relaxed, but he couldn't quite meet her intent look.

"I may not be as worldly as you, but I'm not a fool. Look at you. You're soaked with sweat. Your face is pale. Do you expect me to believe it wasn't important?"

His hard stare cut into her. "Yes!"

She stepped toward him.

He stiffened, his expression completely unapproachable.

"I want to help. Let me."

"Can you change the past?"

"No."

"Then you can't help. I have to go. I'm sorry, Mei Li."

She heard the anguish in his voice, the silent plea for her understanding. In that instant she realized she wouldn't see him again. "Running away again," she challenged as he reached the door.

He put his hand on the doorknob and glanced back over his shoulder. "I'm too hard for you. I'd kill all your softness. I can't do that to you," he said haltingly. "Good-bye, Mei Li."

She watched Michael leave her apartment, her life. She stood in the center of her living room for a long time, numb and hurting. She was in love with Michael Rutledge, and he wanted no part of her love. He wanted to spend his life alone, avoiding any kind of relationship that made demands of him, that made him feel. She didn't understand; she wanted to understand the whys. If only he would give her a chance and open up, she thought.

But tonight she had lost. She had seen it in his eyes as he had said good-bye. Mei Li lay down on the couch where Michael had been only minutes before. She breathed in his scent that lingered on the pillow, realizing this might be the closest she would come to him. She closed her eyes, a tear rolling down her cheek, and wished she could erase his hurt. But only he could do that.

"Dad, you wanted to see me?" Mei Li stepped onto her father's boat.

"Yeah. You can tell Harris for me that I don't take his charity."

"Charity?" she asked, noticing her father's shadowed eyes and several days' growth of beard. He looked and sounded as if he had been up for the past forty-eight hours.

He thrust a piece of paper at her. "Read it for yourself."

It was a notice informing her father of a new loan on his boat. "This is great! You'll get to keep your boat. A second chance."

"I'd rather rot in hell than take a second chance from that man," he thundered, his hand clenched in the air. "He's toying with my life, and he loves every minute of it. First he takes my boat away, and now he gives it back. It's just like Harris to try to play God." Her father scowled. "What did you do? Go running to him and make some kind of deal with the devil?"

"Dad!"

"Well? Isn't that what you did?" He threw up his arms in disgust and started to turn away.

186

"No," she replied in a calm voice. "I don't deserve your accusations."

He pivoted toward her, defeat lining his weathered face, his shoulders sagging. "You did talk to him, though, didn't you?"

"Yes."

"What about?"

"All I asked him was why he didn't tell me about what happened between you two in the navy. I had nothing to do with this." She gave the paper back to her father, tired from the sleepless night spent on her couch, confused by the sudden stranger standing in front of her. This wasn't like her father at all, and she didn't know what to do.

He straightened to his full height, proud, his momentary feeling of defeat gone. "You tell Harris no deal. I'll do without my boat before I'll take a penny from him."

"No, you'll have to tell him yourself. I want no part of this feud between you two. But if you allow your pride to take your boat away, then I feel sorry for you. You aren't taking charity from Lawrence. He isn't giving you the boat. He's extending you a loan. You still have to pay it off." She turned and left the boat before she said something she would regret to her father.

She had to talk to Lawrence, she realized. Michael had been right about not hearing his side of the situation. She hoped Lawrence would come out into the garden for his usual morning routine. But after yesterday she wasn't sure.

At Lawrence's house Mei Li quickly set to work in the rose section. She acknowledged to herself that there wasn't much work to be done in the rose beds, but it was close to Michael's place. She couldn't resist the possibility that he might come out onto the deck and she would see him. She hated the way things had ended between them. She hated unfinished business.

She was so absorbed in her thoughts concerning Michael that she didn't hear Lawrence approach until he called out to her. She rose, brushing the dirt off her jeans. "I'm glad you came out."

"We need to talk."

"I agree."

"Wheel me over there, Mei Li." Lawrence indicated a bench under a Royal Poinciana with its brilliant red-orange flowers draping the tree.

Mei Li looked at Lawrence with concern. He never asked anyone to wheel him anywhere. He took pride in doing it himself. But she did as he said and sat down on the bench, facing him.

She started to speak, but Lawrence held up

his hand. "It's my turn to talk today. You said some things yesterday that I need to respond to. First, I didn't tell you about my involvement with your mother and father because your father's wish was that it remain buried in the past. Even though I was legally within my rights, I'm not proud of what happened all those years ago. Your father is right that I wanted your mother to quit dating him, and I tried to convince her I was the better man."

He took a deep breath as if to fortify himself to continue. "Second, I didn't know a thing about your father's boat being repossessed. I haven't been involved in the day-to-day business dealings of my company for over two years. I spoke with my son yesterday, and he assured me that he would straighten this mess out right away."

"He did."

"Oh, good," Lawrence said with a sigh, relaxing back in his wheelchair. "I wasn't sure John would carry out my wishes. We had a terrible fight. He wants me completely out of the business. He wants total control, which I won't give him. I built that business up. The day I die he can have total control." His laughter held a touch of bitterness. "I don't think my son will mourn my passing long."

"John loves you," Mei Li responded auto-

189

matically because she couldn't relate to a child not loving a parent.

"Does he? What gives you that idea?"

"He's your son."

"Mei Li, you're such an innocent. That doesn't guarantee a thing in this world. Do you know that most murders are committed by relatives or friends?"

Again she realized how guileless she was. Michael's uncle was so different from her uncle. Michael had told her she was naïve, and Lawrence was telling her the same thing.

Lawrence stared through the grove of trees toward the beach. "Something tells me I should keep a tighter rein on the business, not a looser one. I'm beginning not to trust my son with my life's work."

"It's only natural that your son would want to do things his way."

"I once thought our ways were similar, but I don't think so anymore." His gaze swung back to Mei Li. "Enough about John. Have you forgiven me about your father?"

She smiled. "There's nothing to forgive. If anything, I was wrong not to listen to your side before storming off yesterday."

"Then you'll come to lunch today. It's Mrs. Duncan's day off, so I'm a free man. I won't have to exercise. I won't have to rest."

Mei Li laughed. "You don't do anything you

don't want to do. Yes, I'll come to lunch. Now, leave and let me get my work done, or my boss will fire me for being lazy."

"If he tries, I'll put in a good word. See you at twelve sharp. I think I heard Madge was going someplace, and of course, Caroline is at the beach surfing. I'll send the housekeeper on some errand, and we can be alone, my dear." He winked roguishly, then directed his wheelchair toward the house.

She laughed again at Lawrence's outrageous comment. It felt good to laugh after the last few days. Somehow this would all get straightened out. She glanced toward Micheal's house and noticed its shuttered look, like the man. She wasn't going to give up on Michael; she loved him too much to give up.

Mei Li went back to her work, trying not to be too obvious in her perusal of Michael's house. She knew he was home because his car was parked out front. She tried to work up her courage to see him after she had lunch with Lawrence.

"Oh, there you are, Mei Li." Madge hurried toward her. "I want an arrangement of orchids for the living room this afternoon. See to it right away. I've got to go." She started away, stopped, and turned back to Mei Li. "If you see Caroline, tell her to stay around. Lawrence has called a family meeting for later this evening." Her mouth pinched into a frown when she mentioned the family meeting.

Madge left without giving Mei Li a chance to reply. She had just enough time to make an orchid arrangement before it was time to have lunch with Lawrence. When she was through with the flower arrangement, she was proud of her work, but it had taken longer than she had realized. She was late for lunch.

Taking the vase with the orchids up to the house, she was surprised that Lawrence wasn't out on the terrace already eating his lunch. It was ten minutes after twelve. Puzzled, she entered the house through the terrace doors into the living room and put the arrangement on the coffee table.

She started to leave when she heard a moan. She spun around and raced into the foyer. Her hand flew to her mouth as she gasped with surprise. There on the floor at the bottom of the staircase was Lawrence, his body at an odd angle on the marble tiles, trapped beneath his overturned wheelchair.

CHAPTER TEN

Quickly Mei Li removed the wheelchair that had Lawrence pinned, then knelt beside him, praying that he was still alive. With a quaking hand she felt for his pulse. His life force pumped beneath her fingertips, and her eyes closed in relief. He stirred, groaning.

"Lawrence? Are you all right?"

His eyes eased open, and he looked up into her concerned expression. "You're late for lunch." He forced a smile to his lips, but it was obviously an effort to maintain it.

"I'm on a diet. I thought I'd just catch dessert."

He tried to laugh but grimaced.

"Take it easy. I'm getting you some help."

As she started to stand, Lawrence reached out and took her hand. "I don't need any help. I'm perfectly fine. Just fix my chair for me."

When he tried to sit up, she exclaimed, "No!" She met his hard look with a defiant one. "You'll do as I say. You could have broken something."

"Okay, on one condition."

She was relieved that he gave in so quickly. "What?"

"Call Michael. I need to see him."

"But . . ." Suddenly she wasn't sure if she could handle seeing him; she wasn't prepared.

"Please. Now, before everyone shows up."

"After I call Dr. Benson."

"Fine. Just do it," Lawrence ordered pressingly.

Mei Li went into the living room and made the call to Lawrence's doctor, who decided to call an ambulance because he didn't want to take any chances. When she was through talking to Dr. Benson, she replaced the receiver in its cradle.

Her palms grew sweaty at the thought of what she had to do next. Michael didn't want anything to do with her. He had rejected her help; he had rejected her. He had chosen to continue running from his problems, to avoid any kind of commitment. She had never had to deal with this kind of rejection before.

"Mei Li, have you gotten hold of Michael yet?"

"No, I'm calling now," she answered reluctantly.

194

"Hurry."

The urgency in Lawrence's voice compelled her to place the call to Michael. But when he answered, when his deep voice flowed over the wire, Mei Li panicked momentarily.

"Hello?" Michael repeated. "Who is this?"

"Mei Li."

He didn't say anything.

She hurried on before she lost her nerve. "Lawrence has had an accident and wants to see you immediately. Will you come over to the house?"

"Yes."

Before Mei Li could say anything else, Michael hung up the phone. She went back into the hallway, trying desperately to remain calm and in control, but with each second that passed her throat seemed to constrict even more. She kept seeing that last look he had given her before leaving her house. He believed he had to go through life alone.

"Is he coming?" Lawrence asked, his voice weaker, his eyes clouded with pain.

She nodded.

When the doorbell rang, Mei Li grew taut.

"Answer it, Mei Li."

She moved with leaden steps toward the door, anticipating seeing Michael again, and yet dreading it, too. When she opened the door, their gazes clashed.

For a few seconds she saw anguish in Michael's eyes; then he expertly masked the emotion and asked, "Where's Lawrence?"

She pointed toward the stairs, afraid to say anything for fear her voice would crack. Michael walked past her toward Lawrence, his back stiff, his arms straight at his sides. Mei Li closed the door as he knelt down beside Lawrence.

"I had to talk to you, Michael, before they whisked me away."

"What happened?"

"I was coming downstairs for lunch. I used the lift on the staircase as always. I started down, and the next thing I know, my wheelchair is flying off the platform, and I'm hurling down the stairs." The strain of talking was showing on Lawrence's face.

Michael glanced up the staircase to the platform in question. He knew about Lawrence's aversion to small, enclosed spaces like elevators. Mei Li had once told him that Lawrence had had the lift made especially for his wide staircase instead of installing a regular elevator. "Did someone push you?"

"No. No one is here except Mei Li. My chair didn't lock in. It could be another accident, but . . ." Lawrence's voice faded.

Michael leaned down closer to hear Lawrence. "But you don't think so?"

"I don't know. I don't want to think someone around me is trying to kill me. Please check this out."

"The police should handle it."

"No!"

"It's not my—"

"I need your help." Lawrence gripped Michael's arm. "If someone in my family is trying to kill me, I want to know before dragging the police into this. Can you imagine the field day the press would have with this if it got out? Besides, if I bring the police in, the person might be scared off for the time being, and I might never know until it's too late for me."

"I'm not a detective."

"I know what you're trained to do. I trust you. If it's money you want, name your price."

Michael ran his fingers through his hair. His gaze veered to Mei Li, then back to Lawrence.

"The third time might be the magic number," Lawrence added in persuasion.

"I'll check around, but when I think it's time to bring the police in, I will whether you agree or not. A deal?"

"Yes," Lawrence said in relief. "You're running the show." He looked beyond Michael toward Mei Li. "I don't want you to say anything, Mei Li. This may have been another accident, and if so, I don't want my family unduly upset. It would make living here unpleasant. You know how my son and daughter-in-law are," he finished with a grin.

Mei Li nodded.

"Will you help Michael with any information he might need about my family and staff? Between us he should come up with a pretty good picture of them."

"Yes, I will," she answered as Michael glanced over his shoulder at her.

She could see in his eyes that he was about to deny the need for her assistance when the doorbell rang again. She hurriedly answered it, letting in the doctor and the ambulance attendants.

For the next fifteen minutes there was a flurry of activity. The doctor checked Lawrence over before he allowed the ambulance attendants to take Lawrence to the hospital. To Mei Li's relief Dr. Benson thought Lawrence would be fine in a few days. He had suffered some bruises and a fractured wrist, but that appeared to be all. The doctor didn't have to tell Lawrence how lucky he was that the fall hadn't been more serious.

Mei Li wanted to go to the hospital, but

Lawrence asked her to stay and inform his family of what had happened. She wasn't looking forward to that task—nor the next few minutes alone with Michael.

When everyone was gone, Mei Li and Michael faced each other in the foyer.

"Do you really think someone is trying to kill Lawrence?" she finally asked when the silence had stretched to several unbearable minutes.

"It's a definite possibility." She started to head for the front door.

"I want to help, Michael." She meant it on more than one level.

He stopped and slowly turned toward her, his features relentlessly hard and cynical. "No."

She felt he was denying her assistance in connection with himself as well as Lawrence. "Why not? I know a lot about the members of the family and the staff." She would keep Michael's personal life out of this discussion for the time being, but she hadn't given up on him.

His closed expression descended.

"Michael, why not?" she persisted, chilled by the tension swirling in the air between them.

His mouth tightened into a scowl as his eyes drilled into her.

"You suspect me?"

His dark gaze swept over her. "You are a part of the staff," Michael offered in an emotionless voice. "You were here alone with him, and he is responsible for your father losing his boat."

Mei Li took a step back as if he had struck her with each sentence he had spoken. The air felt suspended in her lungs, and she couldn't seem to get a decent breath.

"If you meant to hurt me, you have succeeded," she said in a raw voice and turned away from Michael. She needed to get away from him. She wouldn't stand there and allow him to insult her. She frantically tried to cling to her anger because the alternative was pain and rejection.

His hand clamped about her arm and whirled her back around to face him. She met his harsh look with her own piercing one. She tried to yank her arm from his grasp, but his bruising fingers dug into her flesh.

"I would never hurt Lawrence. And you can go to hell for thinking I could," she said in a fierce whisper as she glared up at him.

He pulled her against his broad chest, his face inches from hers. "I know that," he muttered right before his mouth swept down to claim hers like an eagle after its prey.

She struggled in his embrace, but his

strength mastered hers, securing her against him. Determined not to let his anger get to her, she kept her mouth closed against his probing tongue, gritting her teeth in fury.

He pulled away, pinning her with hard eyes. "Damn it! What do you want from me?"

"Your trust." Try as she might, she couldn't stop her anger against him from melting. She found herself relaxing, her expression softening under his confusion.

He drew in a deep breath and looked away, then back down at her. "From the very beginning I never meant to hurt you, but I have. I'm cynical and wary by nature—I've had to be to survive. That could destroy you Mei Li, and I don't want that."

"Do I have a say in any of this?" She lifted her chin proudly, her heartbeat a slow throb. She felt as if she were fighting a losing battle. He had stood alone for so many years that he didn't know any other way.

When he didn't answer, she continued, "Because if I do, I choose to take a chance on you. Why won't you take a chance on me?"

He stared intently into her eyes. Then, cursing beneath his breath, he framed her head and slowly brought his mouth down to hers, giving her a chance to turn away if she wanted to. She didn't. His lips opened over hers, his tongue demanded entry into her mouth, which this time she gladly gave. His arms encircled her in a tight hold that seemed to squeeze the breath from her lungs. The heated play of his mouth on hers forced all thoughts from her mind except the feel of his lips and his hands on her, the taste of him on her tongue, the scent of him that filled her nostrils.

"Do you have any idea what I'm feeling at this moment?" he asked, his words fanning the shell of her ear. He bit lovingly on her earlobe and answered for her. "I'm feeling frustrated desire. I want you, Mei Li. I've wanted you from the very first." He pulled away, one hand on either side of her head. The sensuous tether of his gaze snared hers. "You've turned me inside out and I don't know what to do anymore. I'm not any good at relationships. I've never had enough time for them."

She touched his face, her fingertips grazing his lips. "Stop running. Let me in."

His self-mocking smile touched his mouth. "That's easier said than done."

"I never expected it to be easy, Michael. Nothing worthwhile is." There was so much hidden deep inside Michael that it would take years to know all of him.

He rubbed his finger over her kiss-swollen mouth, his tender gaze absorbed in its movement. "I don't want to work on this case for Lawrence."

"Why not?" She could barely breathe the words, for the feel of his finger on her mouth was unnerving. Tingling sensations blossomed outward from the core of her womanhood, threatening her rational behavior.

He stopped his tactile exploration and looked into her eyes. "Because I did suspect you."

"Me? I couldn't hurt Lawrence."

"I realize that. But don't you see? For a minute back there you were a suspect like everyone else. All those things I said to you I thought."

"Did you believe them?"

"No, but suspicion and caution have been ingrained in me, part of my job. My motto for years has been to trust no one."

"But this is different."

"Not really." Michael drew away and sat on one of the steps, resting his elbows on his thighs and lacing his hands together. "Already I feel traits I've been fighting this past month coming back. I suppose you can't run from what you are." He laughed, but there was no humor in the sound. "I've tried and it doesn't work."

"Change doesn't happen overnight, Michael. Don't give up." She knew that if he did, there would be no place for her in his life. His old life-style excluded intimate relationships.

Mei Li sat beside Michael. She wanted to reach out and touch him, but she was still too unsure of where she stood in his life. "Are you going to help Lawrence?"

"Yes. I gave him my word."

"Will you let me help?"

His grip tightened until his knuckles were white. "Yes, if you want. But Mei Li, your father is a prime suspect."

Her breath caught. She had forgotten about her father and his feelings toward Lawrence. She remembered what her father had said about getting back at Lawrence.

"Do you still want to help?"

"Yes. My father might hate Lawrence, but he wouldn't try to kill him. I am positive about that," she stated forcefully for herself as well as Michael. She didn't want to doubt her father.

"I couldn't even be positive about myself, Mei Li. Men do many horrible things in certain circumstances that they never thought they would. Hate, greed, and revenge are powerful motives that have driven 'good' men in the past to murder."

"No, not my father," she said with conviction.

"I hope for your sake you're right. Will you

tell me the truth about your father if I ask, knowing that he might be the guilty one?"

"You have to ask?"

"Yes, Mei Li."

She rose. "Then we really haven't progressed very far in our relationship."

"Do you blame me for asking? I've seen the love you have for your family."

"But I wouldn't lie to you."

"Not even to protect your father?"

"Not even to protect you," she murmured, and started for the terrace doors.

"Mei Li," he said, stopping her.

She slowly pivoted, her stance proud and erect.

"What did you mean by that?"

"I love you, Michael."

Stunned, he couldn't respond to her declaration. When she turned to leave, he let her go. Michael felt as if someone had torn his gut out.

Mei Li worked furiously in the garden, taking out all her frustration on the ground. Since she had left Lawrence's house, she hadn't seen Michael. She supposed he had left out the front door.

Why in heaven's name had she told him she loved him? In desperation she had thought it might mean something to him; obviously it hadn't. Once again she fought back her tears and worked harder, tilling the ground around some bushes.

Occasionally she checked to see if any of Lawrence's family had returned, but the first, Madge, didn't appear until five o'clock. Mei Li had wanted to go home hours before, but she had promised Lawrence she would stay. And each time she had looked toward Michael's house, she had berated herself for being so weak.

Mei Li was waiting in the house when Madge came in. "I need to see you."

Madge didn't even bother to look at her as she walked past Mei Li. "Make it fast, or I'll be late for Lawrence's little family meeting."

"Lawrence is in the hospital."

Madge whipped around. "Hospital! What happened?"

"He had an accident."

"Is it serious?"

"No, I think he'll be fine in a few days."

Madge headed for the phone. "I'll give the hospital a call. I'm sure he doesn't want us coming up there when he could use the rest." She dialed two numbers, glanced up at Mei Li, and asked, "You did make a flower arrangement for my party tonight, didn't you?"

"Yes. It's on the coffee table." Mei Li

clipped out, then left Madge to make her "duty" call to Lawrence before her party.

By the time Mei Li pulled into her parking space at her apartment building, her head was pounding. She felt overwhelmed with everything that had happened to her in the past few days. The first thing she was going to do was take a long hot bath.

In the hot bath water she finally relaxed, cushioning her head on the back of the tub. Closing her eyes, she cleared her mind of everything. For one full minute she succeeded, but then an image of Michael materialized in her mind, and one emotion after another tumbled through her.

She knew she would have to see him again if he were working on Lawrence's case. But she was resolved not to do or say anything concerning their relationship. The next move would have to be his.

When the phone rang, Mei Li thought about not answering, but it could be the hospital or a member of her family. She rose, snatched a towel, and wrapped it around her as she hurried to the phone.

Or it could be Michael, she thought as she picked up the receiver and said, "Hello."

"Mei Li, can we meet tomorrow morning before you start work at Lawrence's?"

Her pulse quickened at the sound of Michael's voice. "What about?"

"I'm taking you up on your offer to help me with Lawrence's problem. It would take me days to find out what you could probably tell me in an hour or so."

"That'll be fine," she squeezed out, making sure there was no trace of emotion in her voice, even though the coolness in his made her feel like a knife was ripping into her heart.

"I'll want you to give me a rundown on each member of the family, the staff, and your father."

"Including myself," she retorted.

"That won't be necessary."

"Then you've taken me off your list of suspects?"

"I'll see you tomorrow morning at seven on the beach."

In the middle of her bedroom Mei Li stood rigid, holding the phone to her ear, listening to the dial tone.

CHAPTER ELEVEN

Mei Li sat on the beach, her legs drawn up, her arms clasped around them as she waited for dawn and for Michael. She watched as the sky glowed with the red-orange flames of a new day. The beginning, she thought despondently. She wished it were for her and Michael, but this was the end. He had made that clear the night before.

"Mei Li."

Michael's low, sandpaper-rough voice sent tingles down her spine, and she wasn't sure she could muster the emotional strength to go through with this meeting. She squeezed her eyes closed and inhaled a deep, calming breath.

"Are you ready? I have a lot to do today, so if we can get started . . ."

She rose abruptly, dusting the sand off her bottom. "What do you need to know?" Her voice matched his in cool detachment as she

209

lifted her gaze. She didn't take her eyes off him.

He was neatly dressed and shaven, but there was a hollow look about his eyes that attested to a sleepless night. She realized this wasn't any easier for him, but she was the best source of outside information on the family, a good place to start.

"As I told you yesterday," he began in his aloof voice, "I want a rundown on each family member and the staff. I'll talk with Lawrence later, but I don't want to burden him with too many questions if I can get some of the information from you." He glanced back at Lawrence's house. "It might be better if we talked on my deck, where prying eyes can't see us from his house." Michael indicated she go first with a sweep of his arm.

"I'll talk as we go. I have a lot to do today, too, and I want to visit Lawrence after work," Mei Li said as she walked past him, trying to avoid all physical contact with him.

She had to get this over with as quickly as possible. Her composure was slipping; her voice was taking on a breathless quality. Michael's presence disconcerted her more than she realized. It was hard to talk dispassionately with him when all she wanted to do was take him into her arms and hold him, kiss him. As in the past, she felt overwhelmed by him.

Mei Li avoided looking at him because she wasn't like him, able to keep her emotions hidden. Instead, she trained her gaze on the path that led to his house and tried to ignore his walking so close beside her that his arm occasionally brushed hers. She stepped as far away from him as possible. But it wasn't far enough for her peace of mind. "Who do you want to know about first?"

"John Harris," he replied in a clipped voice that conveyed his strain.

"He's thirty-four, unmarried, and a workaholic."

"Do he and Lawrence agree on the management of the company?"

"I'm not sure. Lately Lawrence has been complaining about John's management to me, but I don't know if Lawrence has said anything to John." Her gaze finally shifted to Michael. There was a tense awareness about him that indicated he was falling back into his role of investigative agent. "You'll have to ask Lawrence about that."

"John would be a good catch. Why isn't he married yet? Or has he been before?"

"He has never married, but he was engaged about a year ago."

"What happened?"

The path narrowed, forcing Mei Li closer to Michael. "Lawrence thought the woman was

211

unsuitable for his son," she answered, her heartbeat pounding against her breast.

"After his money?" A cynical note laced his voice.

Mei Li nodded. "John broke off the engagement when his father gave him an ultimatum about Patricia."

"How did John react to the ultimatum?" Michael paused at the bottom stair to his deck.

Mei Li stopped on the first step and faced Michael. He was still several inches taller than she and definitely at the advantage. Her gaze traveled upward, taking in his broad chest, clad in a white knit shirt, the strong slope of his jawline, the twitch of a nerve in his cheek, the hard glint in his dark eyes.

"Not well," she answered finally, her throat tight. "John hardly spoke to Lawrence for two months unless it concerned the business. To John, Harris Enterprises is very important."

"More than the woman he loved?"

"I guess so."

"Love doesn't conquer all," Michael mocked, his mouth twisting ruefully.

"No, it doesn't." Her gaze bored into his. "But then, wouldn't you say that's reality?"

"Yes, the cold, harsh kind."

"Is there any other kind?" She turned,

mounted the steps to the deck, and sat down in a lounge chair.

Michael followed and leaned against the railing in front of her, his hands grasping the wood. "For you, Mei Li, yes."

"But not for you?"

"Not in the world I live in."

She shot to her feet, anger reflected in her eyes. "We live in the same world!"

"A world of flowers and sunrises on the beach?" One brow arched.

His taunt lashed out at her, building the wall between them even higher. "No! A world of people who feel love, hate, and even the need to avenge."

"What do you know about hate? You've been surrounded by love all your life."

"I'll admit that I've had more love in my life than hate. I'll admit our childhoods were different. But you won't let love into your life. You're so afraid of being hurt that you make yourself stand alone, declaring to the world that you need no one because it's safer."

He let the brittle silence between them lengthen. He often used silence in conversations to unnerve. Mei Li was determined it wouldn't work now. Her eyes narrowed on his face, a calculating coldness to his fierce countenance.

He pointedly looked at his watch. "We need

to finish their character analyses," he said in a businesslike voice, "not mine."

"Very well," Mei Li said tersely, sitting down again because her legs were trembling. It was taking all of her energy to meet him head on and not allow him to intimidate her, another weapon she was sure was his. "Is that enough on John?"

"Yes, for the time being. Tell me about Madge Harris."

"She's been living with Lawrence ever since his eldest son died."

"Didn't her husband leave her well provided for?" His neutral expression descended, as if their earlier conversation had never taken place.

"He provided her with a lot of debts. Lawrence paid them off and gave her an allowance to live on. In turn she's his hostess when he needs one and manages the house and staff."

"What does she think of that arrangement?"

"She does as little as possible, but Lawrence ignores that. The housekeeper manages the house. Madge does show up at the few parties that Lawrence has given."

"Did you go to any of them?" he fired at her, giving her no time to think.

"No. They were given for business reasons.

214

Lawrence has done very little socializing since he's been confined to a wheelchair."

"Did Madge ever complain about the money Lawrence gave her?"

"No, but then, Lawrence was very generous with her and Caroline."

Michael crossed his arms over his chest and stared in the direction of Lawrence's house. "How come you know so much about the family?"

"Because I'm the only person Lawrence has to talk to. When he was troubled, we would discuss it during his morning outing in the garden. Madge, Caroline, and John have never taken the time to listen to Lawrence."

"So if I want to know anything, I can come to you." He looked back at Mei Li. The hardness in his eyes gentled for a few seconds as his gaze ran over her face.

Though the thought of meeting him like this again unnerved her, she replied, "If I can help, I will."

He swallowed convulsively and continued in his cool, polite voice. "Now, about Caroline?"

"You've been around her. You've seen how she is with her grandfather."

"There's a lot of hostility there."

"She's rebelled against Lawrence's authority ever since she came to live with him. But she's that way with her mother as well. As long as Lawrence let her do what she wanted, everything was all right." Mei Li couldn't help noticing a subtle difference in Michael's manner toward her. He still kept his distance, but there was a warmer expression in his eyes.

"But since Lawrence has decided to put down the law with her and cut off all her money, things might be different? Enough to kill for?"

"I'm certainly not Caroline's biggest fan, but I also can't see her killing her grandfather."

"Can you see anyone killing Lawrence?"

"No."

"Another alien idea to you?"

"Yes." She rose again, suddenly feeling confined in the chair in front of Michael, as if he were the interrogator and she the criminal. "Now it's my turn. I have a question for you. Do you honestly feel a member of Lawrence's family is trying to kill him?"

"I've checked the lift. There's a definite possibility that someone wants him dead, and his family has the best motives at this time."

Mei Li drew in her breath sharply. This kind of thing happened to other people, not to people she knew and cared about. She couldn't imagine it happening in her family.

"Does it really surprise you that someone

could be trying to kill Lawrence?" Michael asked. "He's a powerful man. People like him collect their share of enemies."

"Like coins and stamps?"

"Sarcasm doesn't become you."

"No, that's for you."

She walked to the railing and looked through the trees toward the ocean. "Who else do you want to know about?"

"The staff."

"There's Nancy Duncan. She's the nurse."

"How long has she worked for Lawrence?"

"About nine months. She's his second nurse. I don't know a lot about her. She doesn't have much to do with anyone else in the house. Her main responsibility is Lawrence's physical therapy. She's good at her job but not very friendly. All I know is that her family is native Hawaiian and that she's married."

"Okay. The housekeeper?"

"Annie. She's been with the family for years, started when Lawrence's wife was alive and the children were young. She couldn't hurt a fly."

"That's your opinion?"

She whirled around. "Yes, it is my opinion! She's the only one in that house that really cares about Lawrence. Before I came, they were content to let him waste away."

He pinned her with his look. "And you're surprised that a family member could want him dead?"

"It's not the same thing," she retorted.

"How about the rest of the staff?" Michael continued the interrogation in his neutral voice.

"The rest of the staff is part time. There's a maid who comes in three times a week to help Annie. Charlie works on the cars when they need it, and occasionally there's a man who comes in to do an odd job for Annie. I think it's her nephew." As she recited the list of staff members, Mei Li felt her anger rise. Her emotions were fraying while he stood there calmly, with that remote expression on his face. Didn't anything ever get to that man?

"When there is a party, Annie hires extras according to how large the party will be," she continued. "There's a pool company that takes care of the pool upkeep. And then of course, there's myself. Are there any questions concerning me? I'm here to answer any." She took a step toward him, her fury mounting. She wanted him to react. She wanted to hold him. She wanted him to love her. She wanted him!

"Let's see," Mei Li began in a tight voice, "I was born twenty-three years ago on September tenth, the sixth and youngest child of Jade and Charles Vandenburg. I'm part Chinese, part Caucasian. I love to garden. I'm not a very good cook. I swim reasonably well, but I don't surf. My favorite flower is the orchid. My favorite color is yellow."

She stepped closer; he straightened away from the railing, his arms dropping to his sides, his hands opening and closing.

"I love life. It holds infinite possibilities." With each sentence she advanced one step closer to Michael. "But I've never been seriously involved with anyone until lately. I realized that I'd missed out on something when he walked into my life." She stopped in front of him, only inches away. "Something wonderful and beautiful."

"Don't, Mei Li. I'm fighting to keep a balance to my life."

"And I disrupt your equilibrium?" She taunted, mimicking his earlier mocking tone.

His jaw clenched. "Damn it, yes!"

"Good. Because I feel like nothing is the same since I met you." She placed her hand on his arm. "I want you to make love to me. I want the man I love to be the first."

He flinched away, a war of emotions playing across his face. He turned his back on her and gripped the railing. "I told you once that I couldn't make any promises. I realized in the last few days that that hasn't changed." His voice was rough with suppressed emotions. He was still the same man who had come to Hawaii, who could not make a commitment, who was wary of any kind of deep relationship. For a while he had thought differently, that he had changed.

She laid her hand on his shoulder and hoped he wouldn't turn away. "I know." Her voice was laced with desire, meant to unravel his resistance. "But it doesn't change how I feel about you."

He inhaled deeply and blew the long breath out slowly. Covering her hand with his, he turned around. He drew her hand to his chest and pressed it into him. His heart hammered beneath her fingertips. "This is what you do to me, Mei Li, despite all the logic in the world."

She took his other hand and placed it over her breast for him to feel her racing heartbeat. "And this is what you do to me."

He bent his head toward hers and gently sampled her lips, tenderly persuading them to open beneath his. When he removed his mouth from hers, he cupped her face in his hands and asked, "Are you sure, Mei Li? You have time to back out."

"I've never been so sure about anything in my whole life. I trust you."

His hand trembled as he traced a finger across her cheek, over her mouth. "Why?"

Her eyes shimmered. "Because I love you, Michael Rutledge. To love is to trust that person."

His eyes closed, masking his expression from her. "You shouldn't."

"But I do." She lifted her hand to outline his mouth with a finger. "I can't change how I feel. I don't want to change."

He took her fingertip into his mouth and sucked on it, bit it lovingly, rolled it between his teeth; their gazes were still bound. His sensuous look of possession struck a responsive chord in her body, igniting the fire within. It rushed through her, branding her forever. There would never be another man like him in her life.

When he clasped the back of her neck and pulled her to him, his lips found her slightly parted ones, and his tongue slipped inside to explore the soft inside of her mouth, at first tentatively, then more boldly. The fire in her veins went out of control, rampaging through her body. She melted into him, her arms wound about his neck, and her fingers delved into his thick hair.

When he lifted his head, his gaze seized hers, and he seemed to look deep inside to her very soul. She opened herself up to him, her intense feelings shining in her eyes.

"I never wanted to hurt you, Mei Li, and I already have. You should flee before I swallow you up." The warning vibrated in the air between them.

She smiled, but there was a hint of sadness in it. "I'm tougher than you think. You might end up spitting me back out." Then, not giving him time to draw away, she cupped the back of his head and kissed him deeply.

As their tongues mated, his hand began to work a spell over her, moving slowly down her back to grasp her bottom and thrust her even closer against his hard body. She felt his male arousal, and her pulse sped wildly.

"This is what you do to me," he whispered against her lips before taking them again and again in deep, plundering kisses.

When he started walking her backward, his hold tightened about her to steady her as he kissed her on the tip of her nose, the corners of her mouth and eyes, her forehead. "This is something that definitely should be continued in privacy."

Inside his house they paused while Michael closed the sliding-glass door. Then, turning back to Mei Li, he clasped her hand to lead her into his bedroom. But suddenly he stopped.

"What's wrong, Michael?"

The profound responsibility of what she asked of him hit him with an impact that took his breath away. "This is your last chance to leave while I still have some control left."

Her eyes brightened with a soft look. "I can't imagine you not in control at all times."

He smiled crookedly. "I'm being noble, giving you an out."

"I won't leave, Michael. I want you to teach me about love."

"No one has ever asked that of me. The truth of the matter, Mei Li, is that I'm afraid. Do you realize what you're asking of me? Your unconditional trust is scary as hell."

She pressed herself into him and stared up into his endearing features. "I do. You're the only teacher I want. Do you want to back out?"

He felt her deep trust in every fiber of his being. "No way, lady." With a shaky hand, he guided her into his bedroom, praying that he didn't destroy her love.

He stood in front of her, his fingers working the buttons of her shirt loose. Slipping the material off her shoulders, he removed her shirt and tossed it to the floor. When he slid his fingertips under her bra strap, Mei Li drew in a deep breath and held it. When he pulled first one strap and then the other down her arm, she released her trapped breath in a rush of anticipation. After unfastening her bra in the back, he quickly divested her of it in one fluid movement, feasting his eyes on her rounded breasts. The rosy nipples tautened under his admiration.

Michael stepped back. His gaze raised to her face, taking in the glow of her serene features. Then his eyes slowly traversed back down to the hollow at the base of her throat before finally coming to rest again on her breasts.

"You are beautiful," he moaned.

She felt a momentary twinge of shyness, but one look at Michael's expression wiped all embarrassment from her. She boldly placed his fingers at the snap of her jeans, urging him with her eyes to finish the job.

Inch by slow, tantalizing inch, Michael pushed her jeans down her legs, his hands grazing her skin, pausing several times to caress behind her knee or just above her ankle. She swayed and clutched at his shoulders for support.

He glanced up. The desire in his expression made Mei Li's legs weaken even more. He quickly stood and took her into his arms. Their mouths came together in an explosive meeting, and his tongue plunged deep inside.

When they parted, he commanded in a ragged voice, "Undress me, Mei Li."

Hesitantly at first, she touched him, unbuttoning his shirt as he had hers. She flattened her hand on his chest, which rose and fell rapidly with his labored breathing. Rubbing her hand in wide circles, she enjoyed exploring the toughened planes of his body.

Then more brazenly, she unzipped his shorts and slid them down his powerful legs, pausing as he had to caress. She heard his quick intake of air and rose. Naked, his body revealed a steely discipline with its whipcord leanness, flat stomach, narrow hips, and muscular legs and chest.

"You are beautiful," Mei Li whispered.

"I've been called many things, but beautiful hasn't been one of them."

"Well, you are. Perfectly proportioned. Tough. Rugged."

He held up his hand, chuckling. "Stop. I don't think I can take much more of that." His eyes were glazed with passion as he stretched out his arm in an invitation. "Come here."

She did as he ordered, went into his embrace with an eagerness that surprised her. There wasn't an ounce of fear in her at losing her virginity; she loved him and trusted him to be gentle.

"I will try to take it slow and easy, but it will

be the hardest thing I've done in a long time. I ache for you, Mei Li."

"I want to experience everything, nothing held back."

For an indeterminable amount of time he stared down into her face. Then with a groan he brought his mouth down on hers, ravaging her with new, savage hunger. Lifting her up into his arms, his lips still on hers, he carried her to the bed and eased her on to it. He immediately joined her, one leg thrown over hers.

He proceeded to make love to her with nothing held back. Mei Li felt adored, possessed, and loved as his hands and mouth seemed to touch every sensitive place on her body. She was aflame with wanting him, consumed by the passion in him.

Never in her wildest dreams had she imagined making love would be so glorious. She was sure she was on the brink of insanity. Her veins coursed molten lava, her body blazed with throbbing desire that only Michael could satisfy. Every time she thought there could be no better feeling than the one she was experiencing, he would elicit a more splendid response than the one before.

When he covered her body with his and tenderly urged her legs apart, she wanted him more than anything else in her life. He eased inside her as gently as possible, but the stabbing pain made Mei Li's breath catch. He stopped, his gaze locked with hers.

"All right?"

She nodded, touching his handsome face with the back of her hand.

His lips feathered across hers as he thrust deeper. His kiss evolved into an intoxicating union that made the pain fade rapidly, replaced by a wondrous joy that eclipsed all previous feelings. She was riding toward the heavens at a dizzying speed that made her head spin, her body soar. She never wanted to return to earth.

Afterward, Mei Li couldn't find the words to describe what she was feeling. She hadn't thought it possible for her love to deepen toward Michael, but it had. He had given of himself even if he didn't want to acknowledge it to her or himself. Locked away in her heart, she would cherish that part of him forever.

Michael rolled off Mei Li and immediately brought her against him, holding her in his arms. He, too, remained quiet, lost in thought.

"Thank you, Michael," Mei Li finally whispered.

"I should be thanking you. I've never experienced anything like that, Mei Li."

She would never forget those words; they

might be the closest he would come to admitting he cared. Though she realized that Michael had given of himself, she also realized he still held a part of himself in reserve, an old habit that might never change.

Wrapped in each other's embrace, they both drifted off to a deep sleep. Mei Li reached out for Michael in her sleep and felt the cold emptiness of his bed. Her eyelids flew open.

He was seated in a chair across the room, staring at her with that brooding expression on his face that had come to alarm Mei Li. She sat up, clutching a sheet to her breasts.

"What time is it?" she asked, looking beyond Michael to the window. Dark gray storm clouds greeted her.

"Early afternoon." Rising, he walked to the window, turning his back on her. "It's been raining."

She slipped from the bed and went to his side. "Will you share it with me?"

He knew she was referring to what had made him leave the bed. "I told you once that I wasn't very good at sharing."

The wall was going up, and Mei Li felt desperation deep inside. "Sharing comes with practice." Hesitantly, she reached out and laid her hand on his shoulder.

"I was remembering my ex-wife."

CHAPTER TWELVE

"Your ex-wife?" Mei Li's heart constricted as doubts overwhelmed her.

Michael turned his head to look over his shoulder, his gaze troubled. "I want you to understand where I'm coming from. And I'm afraid Laura is very much a part of that."

She swallowed the dry ache in her throat and said, "Then tell me. I want to understand."

Pivoting, he leaned back on the window ledge and folded his arms across his chest. "I met Laura in college, but we didn't get married until after I had served in Vietnam and had gone to work for the government. I should have known from the very beginning that our marriage wouldn't work. But I hung on, fighting, until Laura nearly killed me and herself driving drunk one night."

He seemed to lose himself in the memory, staring beyond Mei Li at the far wall. She moved to the bed and picked up her shirt. As she slipped into it, his gaze returned to her. Michael watched her intently as she buttoned her shirt; the tension-fraught silence pulsated between them.

"She couldn't take what I had become. My experiences in Vietnam had toughened me, but each time I came home from an assignment for the State Department, I was harder and more cynical, until I completely closed myself off from her. I nearly destroyed her. The last year of our three-year marriage was hell."

"How long have you been divorced?"

"Twelve years."

"Why was she drinking that night?"

Pain rose into his eyes; he tried to mask it but couldn't. "Because she wanted to have a child, and I told her we should wait and straighten out our marriage first. You see, I was always so damned logical. I still am, for that matter." His arms fell to his sides, his hands gripping the ledge.

"There was nothing wrong with wanting to straighten out your problems before complicating your lives with a child." Mei Li wanted to go to him, but his unapproachable attitude was in place. "Don't blame yourself for that." Her eyes silently pleaded with him.

"Blame? I'm past the blaming stage. Laura

started drinking, which she had been doing a lot of that last year, and then before I could stop her, she snatched up the keys, ran from our house, and jumped into the car. I was barely able to get in on the passenger's side before she took off down the street." His features contorted with the pain of remembering.

"After the wreck, the doctor informed me she had been pregnant but had lost the baby in the accident. She should have told me. Maybe there would have been something I could have done." His voice cracked, and he looked away.

Mei Li was instantly in front of him, placing her hand on his arm, praying he didn't flinch away from her. "You wanted a child."

"There was a time when I wanted a child to give what I had before I went to live with my uncle."

His voice was so soft that Mei Li barely heard him. She suspected he had never shared that feeling with anyone, and she treasured the moment. It was a beginning, like the sunrise that morning.

"Do you still love Laura?" she asked, hating her need to know.

The arm beneath her hand tensed, and he laughed humorlessly. "No, I doubt I ever did. I'm not sure I know what the word *love* means. I cared about Laura, and we were good friends until we married."

"You aren't the same person you were twelve years ago."

He smiled mockingly. "No, I'm tougher, harder, even more cynical. And I've discovered I have to be very realistic and logical."

"But you don't work for the State Department anymore."

"Don't you see? The damage has been done."

"So you go through life alone, never trying to see if you could make it with someone else. You're too hard on yourself, Michael. Taken out of the world of spies and violence, you change because your environment has changed. Look at your life since you've come to Hawaii. You think of yourself as tough and cynical, but I've found a man who is gentle and sensitive, especially when he listens to his inner self."

"I never want to hurt anyone the way I hurt Laura, especially you, Mei Li. I'm not so tough that I don't feel responsibility."

His voice was taut, but she could tell by the look in his eyes that he couldn't deny the truth in her words. "There you go again, making decisions for me."

Mei Li watched as he drew his emotions into a tight ball. They seemed to take two steps forward in their relationship and then one step back. His eyes glinted with that familiar hard edge.

"A marriage is a two-way street, and both people usually make mistakes," she continued, desperately hoping he would open up to her again. "Rarely is a breakup all one-sided."

"Do you speak from experience?" he exploded, his jaw clenching as he tried to put some distance between them.

But her own anger equaled his, and she wouldn't let him move away. "Don't you dare shut the door in my face because things might be getting a little hot for you. I come from a big family. Everyone is married but me, so I've seen a lot."

"Ah, yes, you are so worldly," Michael taunted, glaring down at her with a look that would make most people back off.

Her black eyes narrowed. "You're damned right I am—at least about some things. More than you, in fact. You really know nothing about people."

He grabbed her by the arms and thrust his face into hers. "And you know everything about people."

Defiantly, boldly, she met his anger; she wouldn't back down from him, because she suspected that if she did, all the gains she had made would be lost. "I know a person can't live a happy life without needing other people."

"My life was fine until I came to Hawaii."

"Liar."

His fingers bit into her flesh. "You like to push me. Why?"

"Because, damn it, when I do you react with your feelings, not your logical realism. This is you letting go!"

Swearing softly to himself, he ground his mouth into hers, driving her head back until his hand came up to clasp it. The punishing force of his mouth, coupled with his breath-wrenching embrace, demanded her surrender.

"Is this enough feeling and reaction?" he hissed into her ear.

"It's better than your unreadable, cool expression. I can handle it if it's truly what you're feeling."

The tension drained from his body as if he were suddenly tired of fighting himself and her. His hold loosened as the air between them subtly changed. "Actually, it isn't what I'm truly feeling."

"What are you feeling, Michael?" she asked, her breath tangling with his.

His body rubbed against hers, and Mei Li realized vividly what he was feeling. His arousal excited her, and she brought her arms up to encircle his neck.

"Tell me, Michael—better yet, show me."

"A picture is worth a thousand words?"

"You've got the right idea," she murmured against his lips right before kissing him."

When Michael opened his front door, he hadn't expected Kurt McNiel, but in the back of his mind he wasn't really surprised by his visit. The time to give Kurt his answer was growing near, and Michael was just as confused as when Kurt had called.

But when Maddie stepped into view, Michael was surprised. "Come on in." He swung the door wider and moved to the side. "Make yourself at home. After all, this is your home, Kurt."

"I know how you feel about surprises, Michael, but I felt this couldn't be adequately discussed over the phone."

"So you decided to bring reinforcements and not to give me any forewarning," Michael said in a terse voice as he closed the door and walked into the living room where Kurt and Maddie were already sitting down.

"Yes, I need all the help I can get. I strongly suspect that if I had informed you of my intentions, you would have been gone."

Michael chuckled, easing some of the ten-

sion. "I have to give you credit for persis-
tence."

"You don't get where I am without it."

"Okay. Try and convince me. I know you
won't leave until you do." Michael's gaze
moved from Kurt to Maddie, a co-worker who
was one of the most beautiful women he had
ever seen. She was a blond goddess who was
very good at her job. He had a lot of respect
for her ability and intelligence.

But Kurt wasn't going to let Michael direct
the conversation; Kurt had found that it was
necessary in his business to be in control of
the situation at all times, which with Michael
was often difficult.

Kurt scanned the living room and asked,
"Where did you get all these plants?"

"Mei Li Vandenburg gave them to me."

"Lawrence's gardener?" Kurt's gaze narrowed on Michael. "Is she the reason for your
reluctance to come back?"

"No. Remember? I resigned before coming
to Hawaii. You just don't seem to be able to
accept that."

"These are beautiful, Michael, especially
the orchids," Maddie cut into the tension
mounting between Kurt and Michael. It
wasn't something new with the two men;
often their two strong personalities clashed.

Again Michael shifted his attention to Mad-

236

die. "That's Mei Li's specialty, and so far I've managed not to kill any of them." When he turned back to Kurt, he said, "Okay, we've had our polite conversation. Now let's get down to business. I'm expecting Mei Li in a few minutes, and I'm sure you don't want to discuss business in front of her."

"The president of Costa Sierra is dying, and various groups are starting to vie for position, including the pro-Cuban group."

"And of course, it's still strong even though the president ousted them a few months back with our assistance," Michael said, remembering the summit meeting in Austria that had cost a good friend's life.

"Exactly. What do you think of the rest of the president's team?" Kurt asked, lighting a cigarette.

"Weak, not trustworthy. They could easily turn the country over to the Communists if the price were right." Michael wasn't telling Kurt anything the man didn't already know.

"I don't have to tell you what it will mean to the balance of power if another Central American country falls to the Communists, especially one right next door to Mexico. They'll be one step closer to our back door. I need you down there. You have a lot of contacts in the country. People trust you. They listen to you."

"No," Michael replied, the hard edge back in his voice. He felt as if Kurt were backing him into a corner and he had to stand and fight because he had noplace to go.

"I won't ask you to do another job after this."

"The hell you won't," Michael fired back, knowing Kurt would get whatever he could out of a person if it was for the good of the government. "I know you, Kurt. I've worked for you for years. You don't like to let go until you're ready."

Kurt drew deeply on his cigarette, then released the smoke slowly, trying to retain control of the conversation and his patience. "This is different. I know how you feel about retiring, but this is important."

"Everything is important to you," Michael countered, realizing this was yet another one of Kurt's tactics. "Every situation is national security." Michael gestured toward Maddie. "Maddie is as capable of carrying out the mission as I am, and you know it. Isn't that why you brought her to Hawaii?"

"She's never been alone on an assignment this big."

"But you've been training her to take my place. She's not a raw recruit. She's been working for you for six years. I'll fill her in on

238

what I know and give her a list of my most valuable contacts."

"It won't be the same, and you know it." Kurt waved his hand in the air as if to dismiss Michael's argument.

"She has to start somewhere, just like I did. Besides, I've given my word to Lawrence that I'll look into his two accidents." Michael threw the last sentence in because he was caving in to Kurt's special kind of persuasion. Duty and obligation had been drilled into Michael ever since he went to live with his uncle. Kurt knew that and often used it to his advantage.

"Two accidents?"

"Lawrence fell into the pool a few weeks back, and recently his wheelchair didn't lock into place on his staircase lift. He plunged to the bottom of the staircase. He came home from the hospital yesterday."

"You and he think there's more to these accidents?"

"Wouldn't you?"

"Yes, in Lawrence's case I would."

"My time is committed to him until I get to the bottom of this. I've given him my word."

"What about your duties to your country?" Kurt asked, stubbing his cigarette out in an ashtray.

"Don't you think sixteen years is enough?"

Michael asked, angry because Kurt wouldn't let it go.

Kurt didn't answer. "I need you. That's the bottom line. I'd like to use Maddie as a backup. You could teach her the ropes, get her in contact with the people you've worked with in Costa Sierra."

Michael wanted to say no, but he couldn't. The word lodged in his throat.

"Think it over and give me your answer by Wednesday."

"Two days?" Michael felt as if the walls were closing in on him.

"Yes, that's when I have to leave for Washington. I can't let the situation go any longer."

"Maddie, how do you feel about all this?" Michael asked, realizing that he and Kurt had been discussing her as if she weren't there.

She smiled impishly. "You know me. I go where the boss sends me. I've never been to Costa Sierra. I hear it's quite beautiful, with some of the best beaches in the world. I could use a few rays."

Michael tossed back his head and laughed. "If I hadn't worked with you before and knew how good you were, I'd be worried about now."

When the doorbell rang, Michael was on his feet instantly, striding toward the door. He smiled when he saw Mei Li standing in the doorway with another plant.

"Are we starting on the bedroom now?" he asked quietly, for her ears only.

She peered around the green foliage. "That sounds like a good place. I don't think there's a vacant spot in the living room." She walked into the house but came to a halt when she saw Kurt and Maddie. Puzzled, Mei Li looked back at Michael.

"You know Kurt, Mei Li."

She deposited the plant on the floor and shook Kurt's hand. "Yes." Then her gaze shifted to the beautiful blonde rising from the couch, a warm smile in her eyes.

"And this is Maddie Winters. We used to work together." Michael didn't put as much emphasis on the past tense as he had wanted.

"I hear you're responsible for these gorgeous orchids," Maddie said, shaking Mei Li's hand.

"Yes," Mei Li replied, feeling overshadowed by the beautiful woman. But Michael's arm around her chased that feeling away, and she leaned back into his strength.

"Is that all you wanted to talk about, Kurt?" Michael asked when the silence in the room became uncomfortable.

"Yes," Kurt said, sitting back down, completely ignoring the not-so-subtle hint that

Michael was sending. "Mei Li, Michael tells me that Lawrence has been involved in a series of accidents. How's he doing now?"

"Home a day and already complaining. The doctor wants him to stay in bed for a few more days. He refused 'round-the-clock nurses. Madge has to see to his needs when Nancy Duncan isn't there."

Kurt laughed. "And I bet Madge is loving every minute of it."

"You know, that's the strange thing about it. She doesn't seem to mind." Mei Li moved to the couch to sit across from Kurt and Maddie, but Michael remained standing, a look of impatience on his face.

Before Kurt could say anything else, Maddie cut in, directing her words to Mei Li. "I've heard so many stories about Lawrence Harris. Do you think he's up to a visit from Kurt and me?"

"If you don't mind listening to his list of grievances against the hospital, I think he would love it."

Kurt clearly wanted to stay longer, but with Maddie's maneuvering, he found himself being guided to the front door by a smiling Michael. At the door Kurt placed a piece of paper into Michael's hand and said, "I'm staying here until Wednesday night. Call."

Michael frowned but took the paper and

stuffed it into his pocket. As Maddie followed Kurt outside, Michael captured her hand and stopped her. "Thanks for rescuing me."

She smiled. "Anytime, partner."

Michael kissed her on the cheek. "You'll do fine in Costa Sierra."

"Testing my wings, so to speak? I'd feel better if it weren't something so important. Good-bye, Michael. Don't let Kurt pressure you. You deserve to fly off into the wild blue yonder. You've put in your time behind the wheel."

When Michael turned back into the living room, he knew Mei Li had questions concerning Kurt's visit and, more important, concerning his previous relationship with Maddie. Michael wasn't in the habit of explaining himself to anyone else, and yet he realized he wanted to tell Mei Li about Kurt's unexpected visit.

He stood before her and began. "Kurt came to Hawaii to persuade me to do that job he has for me."

"Did you tell him yes?"

"No. I still haven't given him an answer."

"I see."

"Do you? I don't think I see," he muttered in confusion.

"It's hard to let go of something familiar when all you have before you is unknowns."

"Maybe it's that simple."

"Feelings are rarely simple, Michael."

He smiled crookedly, his eyes dancing. "Maybe I'm not a total lost cause. I'm feeling, at least. That's a beginning."

"Well, now that we have that established, Michael Rutledge, you have one hungry guest. Where's the dinner you promised?" The sheepish look that greeted her made her laugh. "There is no dinner?"

"Afraid not. Kurt threw me off schedule."

"I'll take anything at the moment. I forgot to eat lunch."

Michael held out his hand for Mei Li to grasp, then pulled her to her feet. "Why didn't you eat?"

"I stayed with Lawrence. He puts up a brave front, but I think he's really scared, Michael. I know I'm scared for him." Her voice quavered slightly as his arms went around her and pulled her close. "Have you found out anything?"

"Bits and pieces. Come on into the kitchen, and we'll talk over a ham and cheese sandwich. Maybe you can help me sort through everything and shed some light on this whole mess."

They stood at the counter and formed an assembly line to make three ham and cheese sandwiches, one for Mei Li and two for Michael.

As Mei Li spread the mustard onto the bread, she asked, "What have you found out?"

"A couple of interesting things. One is that John has followed in his brother's footsteps."

"Gambling?"

"Yes, to the tune of twenty thousand dollars in bad debts."

Mei Li nearly dropped the knife. She couldn't imagine John doing anything like that. She had always thought he loved money too much to gamble and take a chance on losing it.

"Another interesting fact is that Caroline has a boyfriend who is a whiz at fixing gadgets —say, something like a lift or possibly the brakes on a wheelchair."

Mei Li was amazed at how Michael could take a perfectly normal thing and make it appear as if it were connected to Lawrence and the accidents. "My father is, too."

He caught her chin and turned her head so she could look him straight in the eye. "I know, Mei Li."

"Then you still suspect him?"

His eyes clouded. "Yes."

She turned her head back and stared down at the piece of bread she held in her hand. "Do you have any other leads?"

"Only that Nancy Duncan's family sold

their land to Lawrence's company a year ago."

"Why should that be strange?" She would hate to have Michael delving into her past and trying to find something that might connect her to a crime. A shiver streaked up her spine.

Michael didn't miss the tight edge to her question nor Mei Li's shiver. "Because her family is an old Hawaiian one who has had that land for hundreds of years. I'm going to look more into that sale to see what the circumstances surrounding it were."

"Do you have any hunches?" Mei Li gave Michael the last piece of bread and moved away from the counter to sit at the kitchen table.

"I don't like forming hunches. They sometimes cloud your view of the whole picture." He brought the sandwiches to the table, very aware of Mei Li's tension. When he thought of Mei Li, he thought of the rose and its beautiful gentleness. Whereas when he thought of himself, he thought of the thorns on a rosebush. They might belong to the same bush, but they were opposites.

"How about opportunity? Isn't that a prime consideration in a case?"

"Yes, and everyone had an opportunity during the day to take care of the lift or Lawrence's brakes." He took a bite of his sandwich, watching Mei Li as she tried to eat. "I thought you were hungry."

"Oh, I am." She forced herself to eat despite the knot in her stomach. She wanted this whole situation concerning Lawrence over with as soon as possible so she could get her life back into order. She was worried about her father. When he had heard about the second accident, he hadn't acted very surprised. He couldn't be responsible for Lawrence's accidents!

"I've been waiting for you to ask me about Maddie Winters." Michael felt the need to change the subject before Mei Li retreated completely within herself.

"What am I supposed to ask you?" she asked with a half-smile.

"Oh, the usual jealous things," Michael answered flippantly.

"Like were you ever in love with that gorgeous bombshell?"

"Something like that. And the answer is no. Our partnership was strictly business."

"I can't believe she's in your line of work."

"And the opposing side has a hard time believing it, too. That's Maddie's appeal, as well as the fact that she's a damned good actress."

"Why did she come with Kurt?" Mei Li relaxed and really began to eat her sandwich.

"Because she'll take over where I left off."

"But you haven't given Kurt your answer."

Michael laughed. "It's hard to say no to Kurt. That's probably why the government gave him his job."

"Then you're seriously considering the assignment?"

Michael took his time chewing the last of the sandwich before he answered. "Yes."

"Are you having regrets about quitting?"

"No. Yes. I don't know. Maybe that's the only life I'm cut out for. I'm certainly floundering without my job." Michael rose to his feet and strode to the sink with his plate. He leaned into the counter and stared out the window. "I feel lost."

"That's not an unusual feeling under the circumstances. To change jobs is a major change in a person's life."

"It wasn't just my job but a way of life as well." He pivoted and opened his arms wide for Mei Li.

She took one look at the silent appeal in his eyes and was on her feet and in his arms. "Check out the university. Do the class on South American affairs, and see if that's what you want for the rest of your life." More than ever she felt as if she were fighting his past, the lure of his old job, because if Michael chose to go back with Kurt, it would be with-

248

out her. She knew instinctively that he wouldn't take her with him.

"You know, when I majored in political affairs, I wanted to be a teacher. Then the war came along. Everything got turned around, and before I realized it, I was working for the State Department, using my knowledge for a totally different reason." He spoke against the top of her head as he ran his fingers through her long, silky hair.

He luxuriated in the feel of her in his arms because he wasn't sure how much longer he would be in her life. There had never been forevers or any permanence in his life before. How in the world could he think there could be now?

His embrace tightened for a few seconds. Then, without a word, he laced his fingers through hers and led her from the kitchen into his bedroom. Slowly, reverently, he removed each article of her clothing, his eyes feasting on her petite, perfect body. In turn he endured the sweet agony of Mei Li taking off his clothes. When she paused to explore a curve or a muscle, he thought he had never had to call on his control as he had to then.

She laid the palm of her hand over his bare chest and felt the mad beating of his heart. He seized her hand and brought it up to his mouth. His gaze roped hers, capturing her in a web of sensual pleasure while his tongue drew lazy circles on her palm. Trailing a hot, moist path to her wrist, he proceeded to examine it as thoroughly as her palm.

Her eyes closed under an onslaught of heavenly sensations as Michael pulled her against him. Those soft, tingling sensations sharpened to form a potent intoxicant when he fit her small body against his muscular one so that his legs were on either side of her. She felt enveloped by his power.

Her mouth flowered open beneath his, and she reveled in the new world of the senses that Michael had plunged her into. Their tongues performed an erotic dance, teasingly seductive, as their bodies entwined and moved in a tantalizing duel of lovers.

With thrusts of his hips he backed her up against the bed. They fell, still clasped together, and continued, their hands and mouths eagerly giving delight to each other.

As he sought to please her and fulfill her, Mei Li realized she would never love another as she loved Michael. There was such gentleness in his touch and silent messages, yet she knew he wasn't even aware he was sending her those signals.

And because of her intense feelings toward Michael, she felt a desperation as they made love that revealed itself in her fevered caresses and fervent kisses. If this was the last time, she wanted to remember it forever. She wanted to engrave every inch of his body in her memory to recall later when she was alone.

They came together in an explosive union that welded them as one, their rhythmic movements a combination of grace and power. Each pushed the other over the realm of rationality into a totally different world where the senses and the heart ruled.

When Michael rolled off Mei Li and cradled her next to him, he wondered how he would be able to live without her. And yet he also wondered how he would be able to live with her. Their differences were still there, and no amount of passion would wipe those differences away.

Furiously he hugged her to him, feeling his determination to stay away from his old job slipping. He had never been able to walk away from duty.

"Once, when I was eleven, Uncle William made me muck out all the stalls at three o'clock in the morning. I'd only been living with him a few months, and because I had a lot of homework, I had neglected my duty. I'd only cleaned them halfheartedly. He wanted them done perfectly, and he supervised me until they were done perfectly."

"How many stalls?" Mei Li was aghast at the harsh action of his uncle.

"Fourteen. I finished them in time to go to school that morning."

"Were you ever allowed time to play?"

"No. The work ethic was very important to my uncle. Believe it or not, I think some of the things my uncle taught me are worthwhile."

"Like duty."

"It has its place."

In her heart she realized that Michael was starting to sever his ties with her. She could hear it in his voice, even if he wasn't yet aware of it.

Michael massaged his hand up and down her arm. "You're so cold."

"Just hold me, Michael."

That was the way they fell asleep, Mei Li clasped against Michael. In the dark hours of the night Michael pushed Mei Li away. His body was stiff; his head turned from side to side as if he were trying to deny something. Suddenly he shot up in bed and let out a bloodcurdling scream.

CHAPTER THIRTEEN

Michael's cry jolted Mei Li from a deep sleep. Heart pounding, she sat up straight in bed. She could barely see Michael in the dark, but she could feel his tension.

"Michael?"

There was no answer.

Alarmed, Mei Li reached over and flipped on the light. Michael was sitting stiffly, staring straight ahead, sweat running down his body. She gently touched his arm. He didn't move an inch.

"Michael, what's wrong?"

Silence.

She sat up on her knees in front of him to try to get his attention. Her concern mounted with each second of silence. She laid both her hands on his arms.

"Michael, are you all right?"

He closed his eyes, and his tensed shoulders sagged. "I should have been able to do something," he whispered in an anguished voice.

Her brow knitted. "When?"

His eyes bolted open. "Everyone was murdered! I was the only one who survived!"

Oh God, she thought. What had Michael gone through? "Tell me about it, Michael," she said in a soothing voice, wishing she could erase his agony.

"I had to bury everyone so the animals wouldn't eat them." Blinking, he focused his attention on Mei Li. Slowly, haltingly, he told her the story of his parents' murder.

As she listened to Michael speak, tears filled her eyes and slipped down her cheeks unabated. A mere child had gone through what most adults never did and would have a hard time accepting if they had. Her heart ached. All she wanted to do was hold Michael and protect him from further pain. But she also realized that until he came to terms with his parents' murder, the pain would come from within—something she couldn't fight or protect him from.

"When they rescued me six weeks later, I was immediately shipped to my uncle. He wouldn't even allow me to talk about the 'incident' as he called it. He thought that through hard work and time I would forget. But I haven't forgotten, Mei Li."

She felt him shudder beneath her fingers. She had never experienced such anger toward another human being as she was feeling toward Michael's uncle. If Michael had been allowed to grieve and talk with someone about his feelings, he wouldn't be haunted now by his parent's deaths.

His gaze held Mei Li's. "I should have been able to stop those murdering pigs."

"How? You were a child. A ten-year-old boy. You would have been killed, too. Do you think your parents would have wanted that?"

"I was supposed to be there. I sneaked off to gather some berries for our picnic. I should have been there!"

"You feel guilty because you weren't murdered like everyone else?"

"Yes, damn it!" he thundered, jerking away. He stood by the bed with his back to her and yanked on his jeans. His unapproachable bearing was in place as he finished fastening his jeans.

"I never thought you were a man to wallow in self-pity. What you went through was hell, but you did survive. You lived on for your parents. That was the best gift you could have given them."

"It'll be daybreak soon," Michael said, gazing out the window. "I have a lot of ground to cover today for Lawrence's case. The sooner it's settled, the faster everyone can get on with his life." He started for the door.

"Don't spend your whole life turning away from your feelings," Mei Li implored, feeling her own frustration rising as he walked away from her.

He stopped at the door but didn't turn around.

"Face them head on, Michael. Please, or you'll never be your own person. Today was a beginning. You told me about your parents and your feelings concerning their deaths, but don't stop there."

Without a word he left the bedroom. Mei Li pounded her fist over and over into the mattress. Damn him! She wasn't even sure if what she said had registered with him or if he was shutting the door in her face again.

"How's your father doing?" Lawrence asked as Mei Li helped prop the pillows up behind him.

"Trying to sell his boat so he can pay off his loan to your company."

Lawrence shook his head. "That sounds like your stubborn father. What's he going to do when he has no boat?"

"He's going to get a job and in his spare time build himself another boat."

"But that could take years!"

"But he'll be doing it without your help. That's more important than the sea to him."

Lawrence frowned, his features ashen, his eyes dull. "I don't understand your father. I'm not giving him a blasted cent."

Mei Li's gaze was measuring. "You don't understand pride?"

"Okay, so I can be stubborn and proud, too," Lawrence said with a fleeting grin.

"I have to admit that I don't like what my father's doing, but nothing anyone says will make him change his mind."

"What if I talk to him?"

"No," Mei Li said instantly. She didn't want the situation between them to grow worse. She didn't want her father doing something foolish like he had all those years ago when he got into a fight with Lawrence.

"I suppose that would make things worse. Mei Li, would you get my wheelchair?" Lawrence pointed toward it while looking at her closely. "I'd like to go out into the garden."

She put her hands on her hips and returned his look, concerned by the pallor beneath his usually tanned face and the weak thread in his voice. "Weren't you supposed to stay in bed for another day?"

"What's another day?" He waved his hand in the air as if the doctor's orders were insignificant, but the gesture seemed to take something out of him. His hand dropped back down beside him.

"Why isn't Nancy Duncan here?" Mei Li asked, concerned that Lawrence wasn't getting better as the doctor said he should.

"She asked for the day off, and I gave it to her."

"But I saw her here a little while ago. Wednesday is her day off."

"I got tired of her hovering over my bed. I need a little privacy."

"Is Madge here?"

"About, so don't worry that I'll be by myself for long. That woman has taken a personal delight in seeing to my every need. I haven't figured out what she's up to, but I'm sure it's going to cost me a bundle. And I don't want you hovering about, either. I plan on taking a nap, so there won't be anything for you to do." His voice held some of the old gruffness.

Mei Li smiled, leaned down, and kissed Lawrence on the cheek. "I have a few things to do in the garden. I'll see you at lunch. I'll bring your tray up and eat with you."

"You don't have to wait on me hand and foot, you know. It's not part of your job description."

"I know. But I enjoy it."

"That's what I like about you—and it won't cost me a bundle, either." His eyelids slid closed.

Laughing, Mei Li turned to leave when

Lawrence asked, "Have you seen your man today?"

She halted, tension rippling through her. She wouldn't pretend not to know whom Lawrence was referring to. "Not since yesterday morning. Why?"

Lawrence opened his eyes and looked straight at Mei Li. "I was just wondering what he's found out in the last few days. Is something wrong between you two? I thought things were progressing quite nicely between you and Michael."

"Everything is fine. He's busy trying to find out what happened to you. See you later." Mei Li hurried from the room before Lawrence could question her anymore about Michael. She hadn't seen or heard from him in twenty-four hours.

As she began to descend the staircase, she caught sight of the lift. Who would want Lawrence dead? she wondered again. She knew he could be a difficult man, but who hated him that much? A coldness embedded itself deep inside of Mei Li. She rubbed her hands up and down her arms and started downstairs.

When she shifted her gaze to the bottom of the stairs, she nearly gasped. Michael stood lounging against the newel, his intense eyes following her every move. She stopped, si-

259

lently acknowledging the aloof look in his eyes. She didn't trust herself to go any closer.

Years of experience had taught him to hide his emotions behind a neutral expression, and he was thankful for that ability at the moment. Seeing Mei Li on the stairs made him feel more confused than ever before. He had told her things he had never told another person, but did that really make any difference in the long run?

"Lawrence was just asking about you," she managed to say in a strong voice while every muscle seemed to tauten to its limit.

"I'll talk with him later. I stopped by to see Nancy Duncan. Where is she?"

"Lawrence gave her the rest of the day off."

"It's only ten."

"She left a little while ago. Lawrence wanted some privacy," Mei Li offered in explanation, amazed that her inner tension was betrayed only by her tight grip on the balustrade.

"Do you think she went home?"

"I don't know. Why? What did you find out?"

"Nancy Duncan's father committed suicide right after he sold his land to Lawrence's company."

"Do you think that's the reason he committed suicide?"

"It's part of the reason. Her father had little choice in selling the land."

"You think she's the one?"

"I don't know. But a few months after that, she applied for the job here as nurse. I don't like coincidences."

"In this case I don't either." When Michael started to turn away, she hurriedly asked, "What are you going to do?"

"I'm going to pay Nancy Duncan a visit."

"I'm coming, too." She began to descend the staircase.

He whipped back around. "No, you aren't!"

The strength in his voice halted her. "But I know where she lives. I took her home once."

"I'll find my own way."

His words seemed to hold a double meaning, and they lashed out at Mei Li, making her recoil.

Michael saw the pain on her face, and his cool reserve melted. He took a step back toward her. "I need you here. If for some reason Nancy Duncan returns, think of a way to keep her away from Lawrence. I'll call and check in after I've been to her house. Okay?"

Mei Li nodded, not trusting herself to speak. She watched Michael leave, wondering if she should go back upstairs and sit with Lawrence. But she knew that if she did, he would only demand that she leave. The one thing he hated most was being coddled and overly protected.

As she walked down the remaining stairs, Mei Li decided to stay close to the house. She didn't think Nancy Duncan would come back, but she wanted to be near just in case. While she tended to the bushes surrounding the terrace, she couldn't quite accept the fact that Lawrence's nurse could be the person responsible for the accidents. Nancy Duncan hadn't been very friendly, but she hadn't been hateful, either. She came to Lawrence's house, did a good job, and left in the evening. Nothing more—unless Michael was right, Mei Li thought.

Michael knocked again on Nancy Duncan's front door. He waited another three minutes, then took out his tools to pick the lock. In many ways this was better. He could snoop around and see if he could find out anything before he confronted the woman. His gut instinct told him he was right on target with this one. Nancy Duncan, possibly with the aid of her husband, was the person responsible for Lawrence's accidents.

The hair on the nape of his neck tingled as he inserted the pick and unlocked the door. Entering the house cautiously, keeping his back covered, he realized that his old habits were strongly entrenched. Maybe he wasn't as rusty as he had thought, after all.

Methodically he searched one room after another, leaving behind no evidence that he had been there. If she wasn't the person, she wouldn't know; if she was the person, he didn't care if she knew he had been in her house.

He saved the kitchen until last, having discovered nothing incriminating in the other four rooms. He was beginning to doubt he would come up with any hard evidence to link her to the "accidents" when he opened a drawer and saw a box of poison. His gut twisted with alarm. He hadn't found anything to connect her with the other accidents, but was this to be the next one? Poison, given over a period of time after a traumatic accident, might go undetected.

He carefully closed the drawer and snatched up the phone to call Mei Li. He wasn't wrong about Nancy Duncan. And as sure as he knew that, he knew that she was planning to poison Lawrence as her next murder attempt. She must be getting desperate because the poison could be traced if someone were looking for it. Since she didn't realize that Lawrence suspected foul play, maybe she thought she could get away with it, that the police wouldn't look for poison as a cause of his death.

"The Harris residence."

"Mei Li, this is Michael."

"Did you find out anything?" She hadn't been able to work in the garden and had instead come inside to wait by the phone in the kitchen.

"I'm at Nancy Duncan's house right now. I didn't find anything that could connect her with the accidents."

"Then she didn't do them," she said, partly relieved that the accidents might really be accidents and partly upset because it meant things were still unsettled.

"I didn't say that. I have found a box of poison, opened, with some of the poison gone."

Mei Li gasped. "You think she's poisoning Lawrence?"

"That's a definite possibility. Have you noticed any symptoms since he came home from the hospital?"

"Well, I noticed this morning that Lawrence hasn't bounced back as fast as I thought he would. He's tired most of the time, but I thought it was due to the accident."

"Could be. Don't let him eat anything for lunch. I'll be there in twenty minutes."

Mei Li glanced over at the tray she had just

finished setting with the lunch that Annie had left for him. "But Nancy Duncan isn't here."

"She was this morning."

"Fine. I'll delay going upstairs." When Michael hung up, Mei Li replaced the receiver in its cradle. An uneasy feeling was taking hold. She remembered that Nancy had stopped off in the kitchen before leaving— Mei Li had run into Nancy coming out of the kitchen as she was going up to see Lawrence.

Looking at the tray, Mei Li felt her stomach constrict. She had been about to share Lawrence's food with him. She began to pace the large kitchen, her hands twisting together, her gaze constantly darting to the clock over the stove. The minutes inched by until Mei Li's nerves were frayed.

After what seemed like an eternity, Michael entered the kitchen. He paused as their gazes linked across the room.

Mei Li swallowed to coat her dry throat and said, "That's his tray."

He broke eye contact with her and walked to the counter to inspect the tray. "Would there be any way Nancy Duncan would know what Lawrence was going to eat today?"

"Yes. Lawrence is a creature of habit. He eats the same thing every day for lunch. A salad with oil and vinegar dressing, iced tea, and a sandwich."

"Which makes it very convenient for someone to get to him."

Mei Li doubted Michael did anything the same way twice. He would have learned long ago not to in order to survive in the violent world he knew.

"I'm going to have this checked out. Go up and tell Lawrence that you dropped his lunch tray and that you'll have to fix him something else."

"What should I fix him? I have no idea if anything else has been poisoned."

"Go over to my house and use my food. Don't let anyone else know what you're doing."

"Michael, I may have had a few cooking lessons from you, but I can't fix Lawrence a decent meal. I'm too nervous."

He smiled for the first time that day. "Sure you can. Make it simple. I have the makings for a sandwich."

Mei Li waited until Michael had bagged up the food and left the house before she headed up the stairs to Lawrence's room. When she entered, she had expected Lawrence to be waiting impatiently for his lunch, but he was sleeping. His face was still unusually pale.

She started to leave the room when Lawrence whispered, "I'm awake. Come in, Mei Li."

She walked to the chair by his bed and sat down.

"Where's my lunch?" He didn't move to sit up.

"I dropped your tray. I came up to tell you that I'll fix you another and bring it up."

Lawrence shook his head. "No. Don't."

"I promise my cooking has improved. I can manage a sandwich at least."

A faint smile touched his lips. "That's not it. I'm not very hungry."

"Okay. Then I'll sit here with you and talk."

"No, I'd rather sleep. I'm just not up to it."

Her throat closed. "I understand. I'll come back later when you're feeling better."

His eyes drifted closed. "Fine, Mei Li."

When Michael strolled into Lawrence's room that evening, he found Lawrence and Mei Li talking. He held the report on the food in his hands. The police were booking Nancy Duncan for attempted murder.

"You have news for me?" Lawrence asked as Michael approached the bed.

"Yes, Nancy Duncan was behind the accidents. I had evidence that she was poisoning you, so the police questioned her. She finally admitted to trying to kill you."

"Why?"

"Because she holds you and your company

267

responsible for her father committing suicide." Michael laid the report on the bed in front of Lawrence. "Here are the findings on the food you would have eaten for lunch. There was enough poison in it that in a few days you would have died. She had been giving you doses for the last few days. That was the reason you weren't feeling better since you came home from the hospital. She was hoping everyone would think that you just didn't recover from your accident."

Lawrence skimmed through the report, then looked up at Mei Li. "You knew about this?"

She nodded.

"Why didn't you tell me about the lunch?"

"Because we weren't sure. I didn't want to upset you any more than you already have been."

Lawrence sagged back against the pillows. "Thank God it wasn't a member of my family. Now I can get busy and clean house. There are going to be some changes around here." His voice grew stronger, as if the news had rejuvenated him. "Name your price, Michael. You've given me back my peace of mind."

"There's no price. Consider it a favor done for a friend. Now, if you'll excuse me, I have some things to see about at home." Before

Mei Li could stop him, Michael left the room as quickly and silently as he had entered.

Lawrence looked at the door that Michael had closed and then at Mei Li. "You don't have to spend this evening talking to me. I'm sure you can find some young, attractive man to talk to." He looked pointedly at the door, but when Mei Li didn't rise, he continued. "Leave me. Send in my son. There is a matter of some gambling debts that needs to be discussed."

"Lawrence, you should rest and wait—"

"No! When something is important, you don't leave it until later. Go on."

"Okay," Mei Li said with a laugh.

It didn't take her long to find John and give him his father's message. He didn't look pleased by the summons, and Mei Li suspected he would come away from the meeting looking even less happy.

She gathered up her things and was starting to get into her car when she caught sight of the lights on in Michael's house. Lawrence's words came back to haunt her.

When something is important, you don't leave it until later.

Her future and Michael were two very important matters, and it was about time some things were settled between them. She slammed her car door and marched over to Michael's house.

She lifted her hand to knock, then hesitated. He had hardly acknowledged her presence in Lawrence's bedroom earlier. Maybe she should give him some distance and let him wrestle with his demons alone.

No! She loved him and wanted to help. She didn't want him to face things alone. He had for too long.

With force she pounded on his front door. When he opened the door a minute later, they stood staring at each other, neither quite sure what to say.

"May I come in?" Mei Li asked finally.

Michael glanced over his shoulder, then shrugged and stepped aside.

Mei Li walked into the house, halting when she saw his luggage near the front door. She pivoted and gave him a questioning look.

"I don't have long. I have a plane to catch."

His cold words washed over her in numbing waves. She glanced back at his luggage, then about the living room. He was leaving Hawaii for good. A band pulled tight around her chest, threatening to squeeze the last breath from her. She inhaled a breath, then another, trying to fill her burning lungs.

"You're going back to Washington? To your old job?"

The hard line of his jaw strengthened. "Yes. I'm meeting Kurt at the airport."

"Why were you leaving without saying good-bye?"

"I'm not very good at good-byes."

"What happened between us meant that little to you?"

Her dark eyes reflected the awful pain she was feeling, and Michael could barely hold still. He wanted to hold her and soothe away the pain he had caused. But in the last few days he had come to realize that he wasn't the right man for Mei Li. He masked his emotions behind an aloof facade and replied, "It meant a great deal. I would be lying to say otherwise."

"Then why were you running away without a word?"

"I wrote you a letter."

"A letter? Is that all that the time we spent together boils down to? A piece of paper?"

"I've faced guns before, but I couldn't bring myself to face you and tell you my decision to return to Washington. I can't run away from the world I've known all my life. I have a duty to Kurt and the government that I can't ignore."

"What happens after the duty is over? When do you fulfill your duty to yourself?"

"I don't have those answers." His composure wavered. He wanted to feel her in his arms one more time, but he didn't move toward her. He ached to kiss her, to make love to her, something he could hold on to and treasure in the dark hours of all the lonely nights to come.

"Maybe you should take the time to find out those answers."

"I'm just not capable of loving you the way you need to be loved, Mei Li."

"How do you know? Have you given yourself a chance to find out?"

"I can't change enough for you."

"Don't you understand? I don't want you to change for me. I love *you*, Michael, not some figment of my imagination that I'm trying to shape into reality." Looking into his roughly hewn features, Mei Li felt shattered. She wanted to cry, but her emotions were walled up tight.

"I have to leave, Mei Li." It took a supreme effort to keep desperation from sounding in his voice. "Take back any plants you want. I wasn't sure what to do with them." He picked up his luggage and headed for the door.

Ramrod straight, Mei Li stood in Kurt's hallway with an aching void inside her. The sound of Michael's car starting broke the dam on her emotions, and one tear, then another, slid down her cheeks until she couldn't stop the flow.

CHAPTER FOURTEEN

"Go home!" Maddie declared to the pacing Michael.

Michael stopped and looked over his shoulder at her, one eyebrow arched.

"Go back to Hawaii, Michael Rutledge. That's where you belong. You've done all you can here. It's a wait-and-see game now."

He turned slowly to face Maddie but didn't say anything.

Exasperated by his silence, she stood and said, "I've watched you for the last few weeks. You're like a caged animal, pacing, tense all the time. This isn't you anymore." She swept her arm wide to indicate the hotel room in Costa Sierra that they used as a base of operations. "I can finish up here, and you know it. Besides, one of us should report back to Kurt in person."

"You go back," he immediately retorted, but his voice didn't hold any conviction.

"No. You should go. Your mind isn't here in Costa Sierra, and that could prove dangerous to you or me. We both know that."

Repeatedly he combed his fingers through his hair, acknowledging the truth in Maddie's words. This cat-and-mouse game *wasn't* him anymore. But he didn't know if Mei Li and Hawaii were for him, either.

"Look, you did what Kurt wanted. You've done your duty. Now don't you think it's time you started to live for yourself?"

Michael laughed, shaking his head. "Mei Li said almost the same thing to me."

"She's right. And she's right for you."

"You hardly know her."

"I'm a quick judge of character. I've also seen the change in you. I like it. When we've been on an assignment in the past, we've rarely talked. These last few weeks we've talked more than in the six years we worked together. She's opened you up."

And he felt as if he were bleeding. The pain he had felt since leaving Hawaii was still raw, tearing him into pieces.

"Report to Kurt in Washington. Finish the job because I know you have to, but then walk away from Kurt and never look back. Don't let him talk you into staying."

"Maddie, did anyone ever tell you what a wonderful woman you are?"

"You know the routine. I'm never in any one place long enough to establish a meaningful relationship."

"Your time will come. And when it does, don't let anything stand in your way." Michael made his way to the connecting door between their rooms. He would return to Washington, then decide what he needed to do with the rest of his life.

Michael stopped his car at the end of the long driveway to his uncle's country estate. He gripped the steering wheel until his knuckles were white. He hadn't seen William Rutledge in two years, and then it had been only a brief lunch in Washington between assignments.

He had made his report to Kurt and now felt at loose ends, without a job, without any clear decision about his future. One part of him desperately wanted to return to Hawaii and Mei Li; the other part wasn't sure that was a wise move for him or her. He had been fluctuating back and forth when his uncle had called and asked him to visit.

Drawing in a calming breath, Michael put the car into drive and headed toward the house. At the front door, Bates, the butler, admitted him and showed him into the formal living room, decorated in the cool blue tones that were stately and elegant. Michael had always felt very uncomfortable in this room, and his uncle had known that.

"Michael, my boy, have a seat." William entered the room, gesturing toward the brocade sofa.

Michael remained standing.

Shrugging, his uncle walked to the mantel to get his pipe and light it. "Kurt called me a few days back and said you'd quit again." The tone of his voice matched the look of disapproval on his face as he inhaled smoke and blew it out slowly. His gaze measured Michael through the haze.

"I never formally came back. I did a favor for Kurt. That was all." Michael felt as if he had been thrust back in time to the day he had turned fourteen. He could still vividly remember standing before his uncle and defending his reason for not wanting to go to a military academy.

"Oh, come now. We both know that's where you belong. Not someplace like Hawaii, beach bumming." William's thin face pinched into a deeper frown.

Michael ground his teeth together and forced himself to remain quiet. The only people who could provoke his anger were his uncle—and Mei Li.

"I didn't raise you to shuck your duty to

your country. I was in the army until I was sixty-five."

"And you think I should be an agent until a younger one outruns me one day and eliminates me from the game. Is that your idea of duty?"

"When you can no longer work in the field, there are other jobs you can perform. Come, we'll talk some more over lunch." Without waiting for Michael, William walked briskly from the room, sure that Michael would follow his command.

Michael glanced about him. The cold perfection of the room reflected the atmosphere of the rest of the mansion. Large and lifeless, he thought. Would this be him in twenty years? Surrounded by material things that didn't mean a damned thing?

Michael knew his uncle was in the opulent dining room, seated at the table for twelve. Never in all the years that he had lived with William had they eaten anyplace else. As Michael entered the dining room and took his appointed chair, he longed for those cozy dinners with Mei Li in Kurt's kitchen or on the deck.

William waited until Bates had served the first course before saying, "I have several connections in the government. If you think you're too old for that particular job, I'm sure we can come up with one that will suit your expertise. For instance, I know there's an interesting one at the Justice Department. Not as much action, but—"

"Just for curiosity's sake, do I have any say in what job I'm to take?" Michael cut in sarcastically. In the end he hadn't, concerning the military academy.

"That tone of voice doesn't become you."

"And I'm not a child anymore. I make my own decisions about what I'm going to do with *my* life," Michael retorted.

"I'm only looking out for your welfare."

"Bull! You're looking out for yours. It won't look as good to the group of retired generals you meet every Friday that I'm working as a teacher or whatever I choose outside the government." Michael rose and threw his napkin onto the table. "It bothered you like hell that I quit the army. You were somewhat pacified when I went to work for the State Department, but never totally. I think you would have been happiest if I'd been killed in the line of duty."

"Michael, how dare you—"

"I dare because it's the truth. You didn't want me when I was ten, so don't pretend you care about my welfare now."

"I did my best. I had been a bachelor all my

life and didn't know the first thing about a child."

Michael's fingers dug into the wood on the back of the chair. "Love. That's all it would have taken. I needed to be loved and told everything would be all right. Instead, I was shown duty and your brand of obedience. I was told it wasn't manly to grieve for my parents, to cry and let out some of my emotions." Michael pivoted and strode toward the door.

"I'm not finished with you! Where do you think you're going?"

Halting, Michael turned around. "Where I should have never left in the first place. Thank God I've finally found someone who understands me, needs me, and above all, loves me for myself. That's something you wouldn't understand and have missed in your life. If she'll have me back, I'm not going to make the same mistake."

Without another word, Michael left, having finally realized just what he would miss if he walked away from Mei Li. He prayed to God that she would take him back, that he hadn't ruined it by leaving a few weeks before. He hated to think how empty and alone he would be without Mei Li, like the house he had grown up in, like his uncle, a caricature of a human being.

Mei Li sat on the edge of the beach, her legs drawn up to her with her arms about them. She stared at the waves crashing against the sand. The rhythmic sound of the ocean and the salty tang of the air soothed her troubled soul. She emptied her mind of all thoughts, as she had tried to do every day at sunrise. This time before the day began was the only time she was at peace with herself, the only time she didn't think about Michael.

"Mei Li," Lawrence called to her.

She twisted about and watched as Lawrence wheeled himself to the end of the stone path and waited for her to join him. Rising, she brushed the sand off and entered the shade of the ironwoods.

"What are you doing down here?" she asked, surprised to see Lawrence outside so early.

"Altering my routine."

"Why?"

"Michael's advice."

"When?" Just the mere mention of Michael's name sent her heartbeat racing.

"He called from Washington with a few cautionary words of advice."

Try as she might to forget him, she knew she would give anything to hear his voice over the telephone. Why couldn't he call her?

281

"He told me not to get too settled in any one routine. He advised me to keep people guessing, especially as to what I'm going to do and where I'm going to be. Not bad advice, if I do say so myself. You should see my family now. They're not sure of anything."

"Does Caroline like her new job?"

Lawrence laughed. "No, but she'll learn the business from the ground up. One day she'll thank me. Right now she thinks she should start at the top."

"Oh, by the way, Dad found someone to buy the boat. And would you believe it, that person wants Dad to run the boat as a charter for him? The man is going to put some more money into the boat and fix it up like it should be. You wouldn't by any chance be responsible for this new arrangement?"

"Do you think your father would agree to it if I was?" he asked, not meeting her gaze.

"No, not unless you went through a third party and he wasn't aware of your involvement."

Lawrence held up his hand as if he were swearing in a court of law. "I promise you I'm not involved." He began turning his wheelchair around to head back toward the house. "Now, to throw everyone completely off guard, I'm going to enjoy a ride into Honolulu and visit the office."

"To keep John hopping?"

Lawrence winked. "You bet."

Laughing, Mei Li shook her head. "I think I actually feel sorry for John."

As Lawrence disappeared, Mei Li released a deep sigh and moved back toward the beach. She had a lot of work to do, but her heart wasn't in it. It hadn't been since the day that Michael had left for Washington and his old life. Why couldn't she have been enough for him?

As she thought about Michael, her chest tightened. Was he in the middle of a dangerous assignment? Would he be killed one day fighting undercover for his country? He could be dead right now, and she would never know it. Her heart constricted at the thought; her eyes closed on the perfect day in paradise.

There was something different. Mei Li felt it deep within. She wasn't alone, and yet there hadn't been any detectable sound or movement. When she opened her eyes, they widened in surprise.

Michael was jogging toward her from Kurt's house. She was dreaming. She had imagined him coming back to her so many times that now she was finally going crazy. She backed away from the mirage.

"Mei Li!"

It talked.

She squeezed her eyes closed and stood rigid on the beach.

A hand touched her, and she felt warm flesh against hers. Her eyelids flew open, and there standing in front of her was Michael.

"Are you all right, Mei Li?"

"I'm not sure. Are you a figment of my imagination?"

He smiled crookedly. "I'll let you be the judge."

He scooped her up into his arms and crushed her against his hard chest. His mouth came down to smother her words.

If she was going crazy, she hoped it continued forever. Her arms went around his neck, and she clung to him as his tongue parted her lips and delved inside, tasting and sampling her sweetness.

A long moment later he lifted his mouth and held her head still as his eyes drank in her beauty. "My God, woman, I've missed you."

She ran her hands down his back, over his body, enjoying the luxury of feeling him again. "If you are a figment of my imagination, it's the best dream I've ever had. Just don't wake me. Hold me. Kiss me."

His brow creased. "You aren't going to reproach me for going away?"

"Why should I? You felt at the time that that was the right thing for you to do. I love you. I don't play games, Michael. Are you going to stay?"

"The last few weeks have been the longest weeks of my life. A herd of wild elephants couldn't get me away from you now."

She brought her hands up to frame his face. "Are you sure, Michael? Because I want all of you, the bad with the good, the past with the future."

"I'm very sure about one thing: I love you, but above all else, Mei Li, I trust you with my life. I've never said that to another person."

Tears shimmered in her dark, almond-shaped eyes. One tear after another rolled down her cheeks.

"Why are you crying? Aren't you happy?"

"Yes, ecstatically. But I never thought I'd hear you say that you trusted me. I knew you loved me, but to give me your trust is the greatest gift you could ever give me." She drew him toward her and kissed him long and hard, showing her appreciation the best way she knew.

"If we stay here much longer, I'm going to ravish you right here on the beach."

"That would certainly shake up a few people. Do you have a place in mind?"

"Yes." He grabbed her hand and ran, pulling her along toward Kurt's house.

Inside, Mei Li took a moment to catch her

breath. She glanced about at the sterile-looking room.

"The first thing I noticed when I came in last night was that the plants were gone. I hated this room without them, and I couldn't sleep in the bedroom. I think I've grown partial to green." He tugged her into his embrace. "Maybe that's why I tossed and turned the whole time I was in Costa Sierra and Washington. There were no plants in the room. See how you've made your way into my life? If I didn't come back, I would never have another night's sleep."

"But you're a man of action. You've taken care of the problem."

He started walking her backward toward the bedroom. "You're damned right I'm a man of action. I'm going to show you just how much I love you."

In the bedroom they frantically undressed, both eager and tired of waiting any longer as the elemental fires raged in them, searing them as one, uniting them in their love. His lips were fierce and demanding as he silently promised her what he hadn't thought possible: a forever.

When they came together, their mating attested to their love for each other; they conveyed their feelings in their actions as well as words. There was a new dimension to their lovemaking, created by the knowledge of mutual love and trust.

Later, wrapped in each other's arms, they savored the closeness, the silence as the sunlight streamed into the western window.

Suddenly, Michael yanked back the sheet. "We're late."

As he climbed from the bed, Mei Li sat up. "Late for what?"

"A meeting with your father."

"My father? Why?"

"I'm your father's new business partner. I have to meet with him to sign the papers."

"Did Lawrence know about this?" She remembered Lawrence's evasive look when she had asked him if he was the new partner.

Michael looked down at the floor. "Yes."

"When?"

"I called him two days ago, before I left Washington."

"Why didn't you call me?"

"The things I had to say to you couldn't be said over a telephone."

She placed her hands on her waist. "But everyone else heard from you and kept it a secret."

His lips quirked in a slanting smile. "I wanted to surprise you." He moved back to the bed and gathered her into his arms. "Ever since I saw my uncle and saw what kind of life

I would have if I stayed in Washington, I've been planning our reunion. I wanted it to be special."

"Special? I would say it was more than that." She smoothed his hair back from his forehead, not wanting to move an inch from the bed. "Can't my father wait?"

"Well, it's not only your father we have to see. I also have to go by the university. I start work in a few weeks."

"You're taking the teaching job!"

She started to kiss him when he stopped her with a finger over her lips. "And I want us to apply for a marriage license immediately. Will you marry me, Mei Li Vandenburg?"

"Only if you'll do the cooking."

"A deal."

This time when she leaned forward to kiss him, he didn't stop her. Entwined, they fell back onto the bed and were an hour late for the meeting with her father.